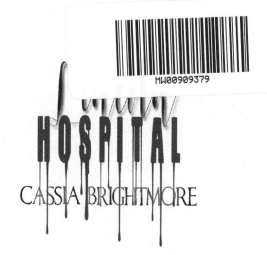

HOSPITAL

CASSIA BRIGHTMORE

Lynette,

Love isn't always
found in the
light -

A C Bright xo

lincoln hospital

Copyright ©2016 Cassia Brightmore

Lincoln Hospital is a work of fiction. All characters, organizations and events portrayed in this novel are either products of the author's imagination or used fictitiously.

All rights reserved. In accordance with the U.S. Copyright Act of 1976, the scanning, uploading and sharing of any part of this book without the permission of the publisher is unlawful piracy and theft of the author's intellectual property. Thank you for your support of the author's rights.

First eBook edition: April 2016

Edited By: Deliciously Wicked Editing Services
Cover Design: © Judi Perkins at Concierge Literary Promotions
Cover Model: Brendan James
Photographer: Eric David Battershell
Information address: cassiabrightmore@gmail.com

table of contents

dedication

To everyone that has ever lost someone special to them. May you find the courage and strength to take that loss and turn it into something beautiful; something you can be proud of.

To my mother, Christine. This story is ours. We built it together and I'm so proud to finally see it come to life. I couldn't have done it without you and I hope that you know that from wherever you are now.

All my love, always.

prologue

On the twenty-third day, he hunted. Peeled away the layers of his humanity, discarded the tattered pieces of his soul. Anyone unfortunate enough to be caught in his crosshairs paid the ultimate price.

Vengeance.

Torture.

Death.

No mercy was spared and no sympathy offered. Those marked for death by his hand were destined to silently scream out his name in agony while begging for their worthless lives.

The walls held secrets bound beneath their tiles. Each step that echoed off the endless hallway spoke of certain death. Once tried and found guilty, the place of healing became the place of your worst living nightmare.

Live. Die. It didn't matter—the end result would always be the same. *You will suffer.*

chapter one

CIAN O'REILLY LET his hands tighten into fists in the blonde's hair as he finished shooting his load down her slim throat. With one final grunt, he gave her head a light shove backwards before standing and tucking his cock back into his scrub pants, ignoring her shocked look of outrage.

"That's it?" the nitwit nurse asked in confusion. "You're not even going to return the favor?"

Cian raised a brow at her in mild amusement. "I have surgery," he replied simply. The blonde, whatever-the-fuck her name was nurse gained her feet and fixed her eyes on him in a glare. He cut her off before she could waste either of their time with useless drivel.

"I find it hard to believe you aren't aware of my reputation. This is how it works. You didn't really think you'd be the one to get me to fuck you, did you?" Based on the pretty pout her lips that had been so expertly wrapped around his cock not five minutes earlier formed, he guessed that's exactly what she'd been hoping for.

It never fucking failed with females. Always had some sort of hidden agenda. Wanting a chance to be the one to sink their claws into the legendary, world renowned, Dr. Cian O'Reilly. Fake smiles and overly sugar-sweet voices didn't do it for him. And he sure as fuck wasn't looking for a life sentence in the form of a relationship. He'd been down that road once before and all it'd left him with was misery. All he was looking for now was somewhere to relieve the pressure once in a while. Love was for pussies and if there was one thing Cian wasn't; it was a pussy. Never again would he give an emotion that much power over him.

Swiping his pager off the nearby table and clipping it on his pants, he shot the nurse a grin that managed to be cold and yet full of charm at the same time.

"Thanks, sweetheart. I want to be paged if there's any change with the patient in room 6B," his tone left no room for argument and without another glance, he left the on-call room, not caring that he left the door swinging open behind him and anyone in the hallway was now privy to what they'd been up to. Let them gossip; they would anyway and it gave the little busy-body receptionists something to chatter about when they thought he couldn't hear them.

His long legged stride ate up the tiled floor as he made his way to the OR, stopping by the attendings' locker room to pick up his scrub cap. He had a routine pacemaker surgery scheduled in ten minutes on his sixty-eight-year-old patient. Normally, a competent resident could handle this type of case for him, but since Henry Smalls was a long time patient of his, he felt compelled to oversee this procedure himself. After all, he was the best. Henry touched something in him that was typically cold and closed off from any sort of empathy. Maybe it had to do with the fact that Henry lost his wife suddenly two years earlier. He'd brought her in for routine blood work in their lab and she'd ended up being admitted with a dangerously low hemoglobin. In the end, she'd turned septic and they'd been forced to sit by her side and watch her slowly pass away over the following few days.

Cian had been called in to consult during the full workup, but even he, with all his skills and expertise, was unable to do anything to help Mary. Watching a man's heart break right before their eyes was gut-wrenching enough to affect even Cian. The utter torture of having to let go bit by bit, day by day, it was one of the most inhumane things he'd ever witnessed. During that time, he'd developed a fondness for Henry and would now not trust his medical care to anyone but himself. It was a luxury that he didn't afford to many people. When his own estranged father had come to him begging for help with placement on the transplant list for a new liver, he'd had no problem turning his back on the low-life piece of scum that had killed his mother. He may not have forced the alcohol and pills down her throat, but he sure as fuck was the reason she'd been driven over the edge as far as Cian was concerned.

Stepping into the scrub room, Cian blew out a breath and pushed thoughts of his worthless father out of his mind. He had a patient on the table that actually meant more to him than just another case, and he'd be damned if he let his despicable father cloud his mind.

With his hands freshly scrubbed, he entered the OR and looked expectantly at the nurse for his gloves. He hated when it wasn't his usual team in the OR, but with hospital cutbacks looming, things had been changing more than he liked. It was coming close to time for him to have another chat with the Chief of Surgery. When he was finally gloved, he approached the OR table and pulled his mask down under his chin, fixing a warm smile on his face.

"Henry. It's good to see you, old friend." Cian ignored the gray pallor of the older man's complexion and the way his breathing was coming in shallow. The sooner they got the pacemaker in him, the better.

"What's up, Doc?" Henry joked lamely, letting out a rough cough as he laughed. "I told you to get one of them young'uns to take care of my old ticker for me. You've got more important things to do than mess about with me."

"Don't be ridiculous. You're a VIP around here, Henry." The anesthesiologist, Dr. Reynolds, came around the other side of the table and started explaining the steps.

"I'll put this mask on you and I want you to count backwards from ten when I tell you to, alright, Mr. Smalls? Do you think you can do that?"

"I'm old, not an imbecile," Henry replied, giving him a weak glare. Cian chuckled and nodded at Reynolds, indicating they were ready to begin. Reynolds fitted the mask over Henry's face and together they counted until he was sure he was out cold.

"Jenson," Cian barked at Cameron Jenson, the intern hovering by his right elbow. The lanky boy's body jerked once as he jumped at the sound of Cian's voice.

"S—Sir," he stuttered, almost cowering under the force of Cian's direct stare. Dr. O'Reilly had the reputation of being brutal in his OR. If you screwed up even once, it could very well be career suicide and mean not seeing the inside of the OR for months. Just having the opportunity to be standing in the same room as him was an accomplishment as an intern, one Jenson knew he'd only earned as it was just a few days away from him writing his Residency exam. The new crop of interns would be descending on their hospital which made doctors like him seem like more of a better option for assistance on cases for the attendings'.

"You'll be closing for me." Cian gave the order simply and then nodded at the elderly scrub nurse indicating he was ready to start.

Cameron's heart did three backflips before settling in his chest. Closing. He'd be closing on one of Dr. O'Reilly's surgeries. Granted, it was only a simple pacemaker case, but no other intern in his class had been given the honor that he was aware of. Sweat formed on his brow as a tiny bit of panic set in. The overhead florescent lights burned down on him, making the room feel impossibly hot.

"Quit squirming, Jenson. It's a few stitches—I'll be the one doing the actual work, not you. If you can't handle a few stitches on your own by now, you're in the wrong damn profession."

Thoroughly chastised, Cameron nodded once and took a breath to calm his nerves. *Man up, you fucktard. If you screw this up, you're finished.*

The entire procedure took less than thirty minutes and Cian was pleased with the result. Stepping away from the table, he motioned for Jenson to take his place. He'd never admit it to anyone, but he was one of the few interns in his group that actually showed promise of becoming a halfway decent surgeon.

Walking towards the door, he started to remove his gloves. Maybe he'd even consider taking the kid under his wing. It might be interesting to have a protégé. The sound of an alarm from one of the monitors had him spinning back. Henry was crashing.

"Fuck," he swore, as she snapped on another pair of gloves and raced back to the table. Jenson had already started compressions and went flying to the left when Cian gave him a hard shove.

"Get him bagged," he ordered one of the other interns, Kemp or whatever the fuck his name was. He pumped Henry's chest hard, glaring holes into his skull. "Don't you fucking die on me, old man."

Cameron shifted from foot to foot, unsure of what to do. He'd barely touched him when the alarm had suddenly started going off and he'd gone into arrest.

"Dr. O'Reilly, I swear, I barely touched him. I'd just started the sutures when he coded. It must have been a flaw with the pacemaker, I—" Jenson broke off when Cian seared him to the spot with a scathing glance. He didn't say a word, just kept his dark eyes that had turned as black as night trained on him as he kept up the compressions.

A chill ran down Cameron's spine. The sheer brutality of Cian's movements was enough to have him scared shitless, but coupled with the severe look of contempt that was now trained on him, was downright terrifying.

"Out." Cian's voice was cold hard steel. He spoke no louder than a whisper but it still had the effect of a gunshot hitting Cameron's body. He stumbled backwards, stepping on the foot of someone—he didn't bother to look who—and clumsily made his way to the sliding glass doors. Once safely in the scrub room, he yanked his mask from his face and gasped for breath as though he'd just completed a marathon run. Watching the flurry of activity from the windows overlooking the scrub sink, he had a quick flare of hope when the monitor showed a spike of life, only to have it crushed when Henry flat-lined.

Cian's shouts to push epi could be heard through the walls. Several minutes later, all motion in the room came to a halt and one of the nurses subtly shut off the beeping monitor.

"Time of death 19:53." Cian barked out. His footsteps resounded his fury with every step he took towards the doors. When he found Cameron frozen to the spot, his icy gaze sliced right through him; almost causing physical pain. He didn't spare him a word, his snub speaking volumes. To him, Cameron was now irrelevant, invisible, replaceable. He was finished in Cardio and they both knew it. Regardless if it was his fault or not, Cian would blame this death on him, for the simple fact that he'd been the last person to touch Henry. Reynolds entered the room and his eyes held a touch of sympathy.

"I'm afraid he won't let this one go, bud. Henry meant something to him. You're fucked," he told him.

"Yeah. Yeah, I know," Cameron replied as they both watched Cian move down the hall, rage present in every step.

Cian didn't stop moving until he was out of the hospital's walls and had reached his car. Opening the sleek, silver Jaguar's trunk, he removed a thick black leather folder; slamming the trunk shut. Sliding into the driver's seat, he undid the zipper of the portfolio and thumbed through its contents. Stopping at a glossy color photo of an attractive middle-aged woman, he read over the typed context beneath her image.

Sally Pope, age 47
Address: 147 Hudson Street, Staten Island
Career: Foster Mother
Information: Arrested and tried on charges of child molestation, trafficking, one count of suspicious death. All charges dropped before trial due to lack of sufficient evidence.

Turning a few more pages revealed photos of several children and a few young teenage girls. Newspaper clippings were attached, detailing the arrest, investigation and subsequent dropping of all charges, which made Sally a free woman. An injustice Cian couldn't stand for. He glanced back at one of the photos of a small girl, barely more than four years old, beaten so badly both of her eyes were swollen shut. She was a tiny thing and was still covered head to toe in bruises. A few baby teeth had been knocked out, causing swelling around her small mouth. The medical report revealed that she'd indeed been sexually abused in addition to the severe beating. Disgust was a bitter taste in his mouth at the thought that this cunt was walking free while this small child would have a long road of recovery from such a trauma, if she ever recovered fully from it at all.

His mind made up, he tossed the folder onto the passenger seat and keyed Sally's home address into his GPS. It was time to hunt. Letting the anger flow through him, he turned up the classical music on his stereo to an ear-shattering decibel and let the car steer him in the direction of his prey. It was nights like this that he shed the exterior that anyone in his everyday life saw. Gone was the professional man with the better-than-God attitude and in his place was the monster that lived beneath the surface. The one that craved a hunt, the thrill, the feeling of warm, sticky blood dripping from his fingertips. The two sides of who he was warred with each other, one with the power to heal, the other with the power to end lives in torturous ways. Tonight, it was time to let the devil out to play. Sally may have escaped a nightmarish life sentence, but she was about the experience a hell unlike any she'd ever known. *His hell.*

His GPS led him to a row of condos and he pulled to a stop across the street from number 147. The information in his folder told him that Sally lived alone for the moment, but would be re-instated to her job as a foster mother within the next couple weeks. He had to act fast if he wanted to prevent her from getting near another child. Considering his next move, he grabbed his phone from the console when it dinged indicating an incoming message.

O'Reilly, what the fuck? You take off in the middle of shift? It was Reynolds. The man was worse than a stage-five clinger of a woman at times.

Calm the fuck down. I'll be back in 30. I'll be right behind a delivery so make sure things are set.

Got it.

Satisfied that things were being handled back at the hospital, Cian put the phone back in his console tray and watched as one of the doors opened from the row of houses across the street. A woman emerged and with a quick glance back at his portfolio, he confirmed that it was the target; Sally.

"Fucking A," he muttered. She climbed into a black mini-van parked a few doors down and pulled out into the traffic. Cian waited a few beats before following, ensuring to keep several cars between them. A few blocks away, she veered off into a supermarket parking lot and after finding a free space; headed inside.

Inspiration struck and finding a notepad on his backseat, he scribbled a quick note. Slipping from the car, he approached her van and slipped the note under her windshield wipers, keeping to the shadows so that any security cameras wouldn't pick up his form.

Some twenty minutes later when Sally came back out, she placed her groceries in the trunk and then rounded the vehicle and paused before opening the driver's side door. Grabbing the note from the windshield, she opened it and even from across the parking lot, Cian could feel her terror at reading the words. The paper slipped from her fingers and she started to run as Cian simultaneously pulled from his spot, angling his car in the perfect position. All it took was a few steps and she flew up over the hood of his car, landing with a solid thud on the pavement. Leaping from the car, Cian screamed for help while fighting to suppress his cold grin of glee.

Reaching her side, he felt for a pulse, overjoyed when he felt it strong and steady. Sally stared up at him, her eyes pleading for help. Blood trickled from her mouth and her right leg was bent at an odd angle underneath her.

Glancing over his shoulder he saw an employee from the supermarket rushing towards them. "Call 911!" he shouted. The young woman nodded, her red ponytail flying behind her as she dashed back inside the store to do as he instructed.

"I'm a doctor," he told Sally as he turned his attention back to her. "Don't worry. I'm going to make sure you get exactly where you need to be." Adrenaline pumped through his veins as he mentally prepared for what was to come. He called forward the image of the abused children, the missing teenage girls and used those reminders to push himself forward with what he was about to do. This woman was a disgrace, a disgusting excuse for a human and needed to be punished—his way, since the judicial system had once again failed to do its job.

Hearing the sirens in the distance, he reacted swiftly and pulled a needle from his pocket. Removing the cap, he expertly slid the pre-filled dose of the perfect amount of potassium chloride into her skin and re-pocketed the needle before the young cashier joined them.

Sally's mouth had formed an 'O' of surprise as she struggled to find the breath to shed light on what Cian had just done. "H—h—he," she gurgled, trying and failing to lift an arm to point accusingly at him.

"Yes, ma'am, I know. It was me that hit you, but you came out of nowhere, tearing across the parking lot. I'm very sorry, but there was no way I could have stopped." Cian interjected smoothly over top of Sally's attempts to expose him.

"I saw, Mister. I saw from the window. She ran in front of the car," the young girl's green eyes were wide with excited fear.

"Yes, she did. Give me that apron you're wearing," he ordered and once she'd obeyed, he tore a strip off it and used it to bind a bleeding gash at Sally's elbow. The remaining parts of fabric he rolled into a ball and tucked under her head in a showcased attempt to make her more comfortable.

As if on cue, the ambulance pulled into the parking lot and the paramedics rushed to their side. Cian stepped back to give them room and announced that he'd check her car for her personal belongings. Heading towards the mini-van, he scooped down discreetly and swiped the forgotten note from the ground and quickly put it in his pocket. He snatched Sally's purse from where she'd dropped it and returned just as the paramedics were finishing up their initial assessment. Sally's breathing had sped up and the portable monitor's alarm started going off just as Cian dropped to his knees beside her.

"She's going into cardiac arrest. Get the ECG machine and get ready to push morphine," he ordered, glaring when neither one of the male paramedics moved. "Are you fucking deaf? Let's get moving!"

"Who are you?" the first male asked. This one was cocky as all fuck, a big beefy African American with tattoos climbing down his neck and disappearing under his uniform shirt.

"I'm Dr. O'Reilly. We're taking her to Lincoln Hospital, let's get ready to move." Again, neither moved a muscle and Cian's temper started to rise as his blood boiled. If they fucked this up for him...

"Cian O'Reilly?" the second male paramedic asked. He was a bulky guy as well, although nowhere near the size of his partner. Caucasian with sandy-blonde hair and sharp blue eyes, he seemed to be the more sensible of the two. "As in the surgeon? That Dr. O'Reilly?"

Yes, definitely the smarter of the two. "Yes. So if you've heard of me, you know that I'm being dead serious when I say we need to go now, or she dies right here."

"We need to be careful that we don't do any more damage by moving her," the idiot paramedic began, before Cian cut him off.

"None of that is going to matter if her heart gives out, you fucking dumb fuck. Just get the fuck out of my way, I'll load her on the stretcher myself." The smart one stood and together he and Cian got Sally onto the stretcher and into the ambulance while the other man finally saw sense and went around to hop into the driver's seat.

He leaned his head into the cab of the ambulance and made eye contact with the paramedic sitting with Sally. "What's your name?" he asked.

"Nick. Nick Parker."

"Alright, Nick. Keep her alive until we get to the hospital. I'll follow behind you in my car." Closing the doors and pounding on them twice to signal they were good to go, Cian stepped back and noticed a small crowd had gathered around to watch. He immediately turned on the charm, addressing them as he moved to his car.

"Ladies and gentlemen, everything is fine here. I'm a doctor, a damn good doctor, and I'm on my way right now to make sure that poor woman gets exactly what she needs." He flashed a dazzling smile that was sure to weaken the knees of the females.

There was a resounding sigh of relief and a few cheers and people calling out "thank you!" as he climbed in the car and sped out of the parking lot.

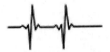

Cian ran through the ER doors behind the stretcher, barking orders as he went. "Take her straight to OR-B." *Reynolds, you better be fucking ready for me.* Two nurses and a resident rushed forward to take over from the paramedics, getting report as they ran down the hall to the elevators, Cian hot on their heels. He ducked into the attendings' locker room and quickly discarded the syringe from his pocket in the Sharps container and moving to the shredder, pulled the note from his pocket and fed it through the teeth; watching as the warning he'd left for Sally disappeared into little bits of paper. *I know who you are. I'm watching you. Get in the van at your own risk.* His calculation of Sally had been on point, she was only out for her own survival and had bolted just as he'd expected she would, right into the path of his waiting vehicle.

Recalling the way she'd flown up and over his hood gave him a sick feeling of joy that he relished. Making her pay was going to be such sweet victory.

After scrubbing, he stepped into the OR and slipped his hands into the waiting gloves the nurse was holding out for him. Everyone in the room was hand-picked by him and he trusted them explicitly. Reynolds stood by ready to knock the patient out and wake them up again at his command, two trusted scrub nurses, Patricia and Lorna, that had been by his side for years were prepped and had his specific tools lined up and ready for his competent hands. With no acknowledgement to anyone, he reached over the instrument table and plucked a tool from the neatly arranged tray. Examining it, his face lit up with cold, wicked delight. The small metal scalpel twitched between his fingers in anticipation, ready and willing to perform his procedure. Leaning over, he brought the tip of the blade to Sally's soft, smooth skin and pressed down slightly. As the first drop of crimson blood appeared, his grin widened. Let the games begin.

Sally's eyes flew open at the feel of the blade slicing into her. She screamed out from her gagged mouth and Cian leaned down to peer into her eyes.

"Oh, I'm sorry, dear. Did you feel that?" She nodded frantically, relieved that he'd heard her and would do something about the pain.

Cian waited a few moments, lulling her into a false sense of safety, allowing her to think that feeling the scalpel was just an error. When he was certain she was relaxed, he resumed his task of cutting shallow cuts up and down her right arm, watching as the blood flowed freely onto the table and then dripped onto the floor.

"Ahhhh! Ah!" Sally screamed out behind the gag with each swipe of the knife, the pain was excruciating, she felt it in every molecule of her skin.

"So you felt that as well. What a shame. Tell me, Ms. Pope, how do you think those children felt when they were beaten? When they were being sexually abused by the men you let in your home? *Children.* Some under four fucking years old. You exploited them, used them to make a few extra dollars. You make me sick," Cian spat at her.

Sally's eyes had gone wide as saucers as realization dawned. It wasn't a mistake that she was feeling everything the doctor was doing. It was *deliberate*. She was being punished; tortured. Frantically, she shook her head and tried to plead from behind her gag.

Her begging only fueled the fire of his rage. He motioned for the nurse to step closer with the retractor. In one clean movement, he sliced down her chest diagonally, ignoring the way her body tried to buck off the table. She was restrained at the ankles and both arms were spread wide and strapped down to the table. Forcing the retractor into the incision he'd made, he cracked her chest and then shot her a look.

"Well look at that. You do have a heart. Pity it's just an organ to you, no real fucking emotion from you at all. Pliers," he ordered, holding out his hand.

When the instrument was in his grasp, he nodded at Reynold's who slipped the gag from her mouth. Sally promptly started screaming bloody murder; Reynolds quickly wrapped his hands around her throat, cutting off her air just enough to keep her quiet. Cian fit the pliers over one of her bottom teeth and then locked eyes with her.

"One of those children was missing teeth. It's only fair you know the pain that child felt, don't you think?" Sally squirmed and bucked but it was no use. With a ruthless yank, he pulled the tooth out from the root, letting it drop in a stainless steel basin. He repeated the motion four more times before stepping back.

"Shame about you hitting the pavement so hard that it knocked your teeth loose, isn't it?" Sally was reduced to almost inaudible whimpers of pain now, and he was pretty certain she'd soiled herself.

"Let's finish this, I can't stand to look at her any longer," Cian said and retrieved the scalpel. With a precise movement, he punctured her aorta. She'd bleed out in minutes, a much more merciful death than she deserved after the hell she'd inflicted on others, but it'd have to do. They were a little ahead schedule on this kill and Cian couldn't risk any unwanted visitors coming into his OR.

When it was over and she was finally dead, Cian looked around and was satisfied on what he saw on his team's faces. They all had their reasons for what they did, but it was never spoken of. Their acts of vigilantism would never be accepted by society, especially in the way they performed it. Some may have wanted him persecuted for what he did, but the simple fact was—he killed people that needed killing.

The need inside him grew with each passing day and when the twenty-third day of the month came around, he hunted down one of his selected victims and carried out the punishment they'd managed to escape. Lately, the hunger to take human life was growing strong and it was becoming more difficult to wait the standard time he'd set out for himself, making it difficult to balance the two sides of his life. The Dr. O'Reilly who walked in the daylight and was a legendary life saver, and the Dr. O'Reilly who emerged in the night and was the judge, jury and executioner for anyone that escaped proper justice for their crimes.

"Same clean-up procedure. I'll write up the post-op notes next shift. Good work." He walked out of the OR without another word, riding on the thrill of another successful kill under the nose of everyone in the building. It felt fucking good, powerful, he was drunk on the adrenaline of it. It was going to be a long four weeks.

chapter two

ATHENA PAYNE GAZED up at the large, formidable looking building that would hold ninety percent of her time for the next several years. Lincoln Hospital was actually two separate buildings joined together by a skywalk built over a main road. The lawns and gardens were immaculate, an obvious triumph of endless hours of work by several talented gardeners. The bright early morning sun glinted off the windows casting a heavenly glow over the hospital. To the naked eye, it looked like a friendly, welcoming establishment. Those in the medical profession knew better. While it could be the place that restored hope when all was lost, the walls also held the ghosts of unspeakable grief. An ocean of tears spilled over lost loved ones would forever stain the floors; destined to never be mopped dry.

As a first year surgical intern, Athena was not naive about the types of cases she would be working on. In order to even have a shot of holding the elusive scalpel in the OR, there first had to be some sort of tragedy. Especially in cardiothoracic surgery. And that was exactly where she wanted to be. It was the most hardcore of all the specialties, but she didn't care. It was her dream to become a cardiothoracic surgeon and nothing was going to stand in her way. Looking down at herself, she smoothed the front of her sensible white dress shirt before running a hand through her thick, dark brown hair. Her Greek heritage on both her mother and father's side gave her skin a year-round tanned glow that brought out the light in her olive green eyes.

First day jitters had her lingering in the parking lot longer than she should. Shifting from foot to foot, she took a deep breath and willed her feet to carry her forward towards the sliding glass doors that splashed the hospital's name in an elegant scrawl. When she still remained rooted in place a few minutes later, she gave herself a mental kick in the ass.

"Athena Payne!" Athena spun at the sound of her name being bellowed across the parking lot. Her best friend and fellow intern, Sabine Adams, was sprinting her way, her coat flapping out behind her and her black as night curls going every which way. "Girl, I'm late, so what the hell are you doing standing out here like you're waiting for the ice cream truck to pass by? You best be getting your ass in there and not considering bolting on me." she ordered as she skidded to a halt beside her and blew out a breath.

"I'm not bolting. This is me...non-bolting. I'm just waiting," Athena replied, eyeing her best friend out of the corner of her eye. She had no doubt that Sabine had literally just rolled out of bed and threw on anything that smelled clean and rushed out the door. Her make-up was a tad smeared but the look worked on her and curly hair was tousled, but could be blamed on the wind. Her stretchy pants and oversize top dwarfed her, but the slouched look suited her. The only part of her that looked out of place was the tan raincoat style jacket that was now hanging haphazardly off one shoulder.

"Is that..." she peered closer at her friend. "Is that a man's coat?"

Sabine blushed, completely out of character for her, and tugged on the ends of the belt. "No. Yes. Well, so what? A coat is a coat. Don't change the subject, Athena. We've got to get in there."

Athena decided to let the matter drop for the moment but promised herself she would get to the bottom of the mystery owner of the obvious men's coat Sabine was wearing. Straightening her spine, she nodded at Sabine that she was ready and the two stepped forward towards the main entrance. A squeal of tires and a sudden blast of a blaring horn had both jumping back out of the path of a silver sports car that came tearing around the corner. The car narrowly missed flattening their toes by inches and then slid smoothly into a front parking space. In shock, Athena stared transfixed as the owner climbed from the car and pressing the key fob over his right shoulder, engaged the locks on his car with a subtle *beep beep.*

"Sorry," he tossed to them in a way that expressed he was most definitely *not* sorry at all, before leaving them standing there gaping after him.

"Jesus fucking fuck. Do you see him? Oh, my God he's a walking orgasm maker. I think I just soaked my panties, Thene," Sabine breathed, clutching her arm for balance.

"Since when do you wear panties?" Athena muttered back almost absent-mindedly as she watched the rude man's departure. Sure, he was dead sexy, but he obviously had some sort of God complex if he could almost kill them the way he did and then brush them off as though they were last week's leftovers. In that one second their eyes had met, she'd glimpsed something in his almost black gaze. Something that spoke of power and authority. Whoever he was, it definitely wasn't his first day on the job like it was theirs. His denim clad legs showcased muscular thighs and a tight ass. The black dress shirt stretched tight across his chest and arms, making him appear impossibly built. Yes, the way he carried himself and his flashy car—that she now recognized as a Jaguar—spoke of someone in a position of rank. But above all, he was a grade-A douche and she hoped they had no dealings with him at all.

Sabine was still gushing on and on about his dark hair and wondering aloud if she could get a ride in his backseat after shift was over as they hurried towards the front doors.

"Sabine, no. The guy's an ass. He nearly ran us over and didn't even care!" The sliding doors closed behind them and spotting a sign that announced *Surgical Intern Orientation* with an arrow, she steered them to the right while trying to talk sense into her best friend.

"Who cares? I'll take it as a hazard of getting a piece of that drop-dead gorgeous man," Sabine shot her a sassy wink. Athena rolled her eyes and together they pushed open the double doors that the signs indicated lead to the intern locker rooms. The room was filled with around twenty men and women all talking excitedly while pulling on white lab coats and picking up pagers from a waiting table.

In the center of the room, a middle-aged man stood calling names from a tablet, scrolling and tapping as people called out, "here!" in reply. Spotting them, he raised his eyebrows and then looked pointedly at the clock above their heads. Turning slightly, Athena took note that they were indeed fifteen minutes late, thanks to her cold feet and their near death experience with Mr. Asshole of the Year.

"Names," he ordered.

"Athena Payne?" she answered automatically, grimacing when it came out as a question. She cleared her throat and tried again. "Dr. Athena Payne, sir. I apologize for being late. There was an...incident in the parking lot." His nod was the only response she got to her lame excuse and she urgently elbowed Sabine to get her to pay attention.

"Sabine Adams," she called out after tearing her eyes away from a blond-haired, blue-eyed stud trying to nonchalantly flex his biceps after he caught Sabine's eye on him. Her friend was as boy-crazy as they came and had more sexuality in her baby toe than Athena had in her whole body. She wasn't a prude by any means, but chasing her next one-night stand was not as high on her priorities as it was on Sabine's. She had goals, ambitions, a plan. Getting tied up in some messy hospital romantic drama was not part of it and she'd be damned if anything stopped her from what she'd worked so hard for in medical school. If she wanted to be the best, the only thing that would put her at the top was keeping her eye on the prize and proving herself as a serious contender very early in the game. Surgeries. She needed surgeries and a lot of them.

"Are you with us here, Payne?" Realizing she'd been caught staring into space, she blushed and quickly turned her attention back to the man calling out the roll call. His annoyed expression relayed that she really was blowing her chance at a good first impression. She'd have to work extra hard to prove she wasn't an airhead.

"Yes, sir."

"Good. Now as I was saying, I'm Dr. Murphy, the Chief of Surgery." Hearing those words, Athena's heart sank. The Chief? This was the Chief and she'd not only been late, she'd been caught daydreaming like a five-year-old child. *Just fucking great.* "I'll be splitting you up into groups of six and then you'll be meeting the residents that you'll be working under for the next year of your internship. Your residents are your Gods; you're to listen to them and if you want my advice, make them as damn happy as you can. They will have the deciding vote on when you finally get to step foot inside an OR for the first time."

The room fell silent as soon as he mentioned the word 'surgery', with all eyes pinned to him. It was the nature of the beast, interns were known to be blood-thirsty; craving the scalpel and the chance to get in on the action in the OR. Surgery was one of the most competitive occupations out there, there was no telling what one of your co-workers would do just to get their feet in that room. It was cutthroat, brutal and cost people friendships. Horror stories and rumors were spread everyday of underhanded tactics that doctors stooped to just to be the chosen one to make that cut.

"Adams, Payne, Sullivan, Barton, Tucker, Breyers. You'll be with Dr. Webster. Pick up your pagers there," he motioned towards the table, "if you haven't already done so." A pointed look in their direction with that comment, caused Athena to blush once again. "Your lockers have already been assigned."

There was a small flurry of activity as pagers were picked up and belongings stored away in lockers. Athena pulled out the white lab coat hanging in hers and took a moment to run her fingers over the embroidery over the left breast. *Dr. Athena Payne, M.D.,* seeing her name associated with those two very important letters filled her with a sense of accomplishment, of belonging. She'd actually done it. Finished medical school and was about to embark on the first step in the journey to making all her dreams come true. Despite all the obstacles, all the endless nights studying and cramming, she'd made it. Now it was her time to shine.

"Payne, Adams, hang on a second," the Chief called out to them as they headed out the door. With a sinking feeling, Athena turned back and offered the Chief a small smile. Sabine's sigh could be heard from the Statue of Liberty and it took all of her effort to not smack her on the back of the head to get her to shut up and not get them in any more trouble.

"Yes, Chief?" she asked.

"Being accepted into this program at this hospital is not only an accomplishment, it's an honor. We receive applications from across the country from thousands of intern hopefuls. We are the most competitive, we house some of the best surgeons in the field and when completing this program, our residents go on to accept some of the most prestigious placements. To be chosen is a privilege, not a right and it's not something either of you should be taking for granted." He let the weight of his words fall on their shoulders, his hard blue eyes locked on both of them before continuing. "Do not be late tomorrow. If you aren't here to be serious, there are quite a number of people that didn't get your spot that would be happy to take it." He turned on his heel and left them in locker room without another word.

Athena covered her face with her hands and let out a loud groan. "Oh, my God, Sab, this is a disaster! The Chief hates us already! And did you see all the smirks and giggles from the other interns, we're laughingstocks."

"Oh, stop. Those lamebrains are just jealous. So maybe we've annoyed the Chief, but look on the bright side—he knows our names already and there's no bad in that," she linked their arms and dragged Athena from the locker room, refusing to let the situation get to her.

Once in the hall, they met up with the other interns that had been assigned to their resident.

Bianca Sullivan, Richard Barton, Clarence Tucker, and Oscar Breyers were the other interns they'd been paired with, Athena had learned after glimpsing their names on the Chief's tablet when he was lecturing them. The group of four stood impatiently waiting for Athena and Sabine to join them. Bianca was a tall, dark-skinned beauty who had her thick black hair gathered up in a bun on top of her head. Black rimmed glasses perched on her nose as she watched them approach. She opened her mouth to speak, but the guy to her right beat her to the punch.

"You're lucky we waited for you. I didn't want to, but she," he hooked a thumb at Bianca, "insisted." Bianca huffed and offered a hand to each of them.

"Don't listen to this idiot. We're all going to be working together so might as well start off on the right foot. I'm Bianca." Athena offered her a friendly smile in return.

"Thanks, Bianca. I'm Athena and this is Sabine." Clarence and Oscar introduced themselves and Athena took an instant liking to Clarence. With his dark hair and warm brown eyes, he instantly put her at ease with his laid-back attitude and open reception. Oscar was the quietest of the bunch. A little on the short and heavy side, he reminded her of the kid who was always picked last for the team which immediately endeared him to Athena. He seemed like a sweet boy and she hoped that he'd be able to find the inner strength he'd need to survive in a surgical program.

Richard was an all around asshole and her dislike of him was immediate. His disposition left a bad taste in her mouth and if he leered at her chest one more time she was certain to simultaneously stomp on his foot and punch him in the nose to get him to back off. Finally giving in and introducing himself to the group, he stepped way too close into her space, causing her to frown at him.

"I'm Richard. You can call me, Dick." Sabine snickered beside her and Athena shot her a warning glance to keep quiet when she saw her mouth open to deliver what would no doubt have been a snide remark about his nickname. Sabine sulked, but otherwise remained silent.

"Well, *Dick*, it's nice to meet you. Sorry if we caused you any sort of inconvenience," Athena forced a smile before giving him her back. "Not sorry at all, you bully," she muttered under her breath. She caught Clarence's eye and he grinned at her, letting her know he heard her comment and approved. With the exception of Dick, they had a good group paired up. Now, with a little luck they'd have a decent resident and the rough start to her first day would take a turn for the better.

"These must be my interns." All six heads turned at the sound of someone speaking from behind them. A pissed off redhead stood a few feet away glaring at them. The name on her lab coat read *Dr. Faye Webster, M.D.*

Shit. This was their resident and she'd had to track them down. There went her hopes for the first day improving.

"I'd ask you why I had to come to you, but you're interns which means you have rocks where your brains should be and therefore I shouldn't be surprised that you don't have any sense." Her black heels clicked on the tiled floor as she closed the distance between them, showcasing her shapely legs in a slim pencil skirt and stockings.

"Ma'am, it was these two that held us up," Dick spoke up, pointing an accusing finger at Athena and Sabine. "They were late to the orientation and then refused to allow us to come and meet you." Athena gaped at him, unable to believe that he'd thrown them under the bus like that, and added in a lie to make it seem worse. She felt Sabine tense beside her and knew her best friend was coiled and ready to spring at any moment.

Before she could defend themselves, Dr. Webster surprised her by looking at Dick in disgust. "Just stop talking. I don't know your name yet and right now; I don't want to know it. Not having your fellow doctors' backs tells me all I need to know about you at the moment. You better learn pretty damn fast that you need to work as a team around here if you want to be accepted. Go and gather up the charts for rooms 17B, 22C, 4A, 33B. You can re-join us on our rounds. Since I didn't see you write those room numbers down, I hope you have a good memory. The first thing you'll all learn about me is I do not repeat myself. Remember that and we'll get along fine. And another thing, if you ever call me ma'am again, you'll be doing chart prep in the ER for the rest of the year. Now, let's get moving, we've got rounds and we're behind."

Dick's stare bordered on hateful as he glared at Athena before hurrying off to do as he was instructed.

"I don't want to know the excuses. Just understand that if you're late again or do anything else to make me look bad in front of the Chief or my peers, you won't be so lucky as to just get stuck on chart prep in the ER. That goes for all of you," Webster added, letting her green eyes fall on each of them.

They followed her down the hall to the first patient room and Athena couldn't help the small amount of pride that began to rise up in her. She was about to walk into her first patient room as a doctor, a doctor that could possibly end up operating on this patient if she was lucky enough to scrub in. Everything she'd worked for was about to start coming true.

Stepping inside behind the other interns, her heart sank when she saw the patient she was so excited about possibly cutting into was no more than a child. A five or six-year-old boy lay in the too-white bed, his complexion pale and his small body hooked up to far too many machines.

"Sebastian Harris, age five. Admitted overnight with shortness of breath. How are you two doing today, Mrs. Harris?" Webster addressed the slim woman leaning over the boy. The dark circles under her eyes and the protective way she hovered indicated this was Sebastian's mother.

"Hi, Dr. Webster. We're hanging in, aren't we, Sebastian?" Her smile was full of love but her eyes held her fear. Fear that she'd lose her child before he really got a chance to live. "You have quite the entourage today," she commented, her eyes darting nervously over the group of interns crowded into the room.

"They're interns, pay them no mind." A deep voice answered from the door. The bodies shuffled and made way for the man as he shouldered his way through. He walked to Mrs. Harris and put a hand on her shoulder and then ruffled Sebastian's blond hair.

"Good morning, champ. Got an update on the scores for me?" Athena's mouth dropped as she recognized the man in the white coat. It was the douche from that morning that had nearly ran over her and Sabine. Now he was here in the same patient room as them. Was he an intern? No, he was too old for that. A resident? Too authoritative for that. Oh, God. Please, no. He can't be...

Sebastian answered the douche's question before she got a chance to finish her thought. "Dr. O'Reilly! The Yankees were down by three runs in the 8th, but they came back to win in the bottom of the 9th. You owe me ten minutes outside today. You promised."

"Okay, kid. We'll talk," he smiled once more at him and then turned to address the interns. "I'm Dr. Cian O'Reilly, Chief of Cardiothoracic Surgery. Who can tell me based on the symptoms you've observed so far why Sebastian has been admitted?" The room fell dead quiet; no one brave enough to answer.

His eyes locked with hers, his penetrating gaze staring right through her. She knew the answer and he knew it. They engaged in a silent battle of wills, her refusing to address him, him refusing to let her get away that easily. Finally, on a sigh, she gave in.

"Heart transplant?" her answer came out like a question and that annoyed her. She cleared her throat and tried again. "My preliminary assessment is that Sebastian is waiting on a heart transplant." She looked at his mother sympathetically, her heart breaking as the woman's eyes filled with tears.

"Correct. And in the time you wasted voicing that accurate assessment, you lost precious seconds. Seconds that could cost this little boy if someone else was placed above him on the transplant list as a result of your hesitation. To be a good doctor, you need to study hard, practice and have real skills. To be an outstanding doctor, you need to have good instincts and enough sense to know when to follow them." He looked hard at each of them, his gaze finally coming back to land on her. This time, a jolt of electricity flowed through her at the contact. There was something about his cold and domineering attitude that both infuriated her and turned her on at the same time. He was sexy as sin and he damn well knew it. "In your case, I'd say you better start practicing those skills if you want to have a chance at becoming an outstanding doctor." His words were meant as a stinging blow and they hit home hard. Her temper rose, and she had to fight like hell to keep herself in check.

Dick crashed into the room, the door banging off the wall as he juggled an armload of tablets and binders. Oblivious to the tension, he announced that he'd gathered the charts.

"Are we supposed to give you a medal?" Athena snapped before she could stop herself. Her face turning bright red, she covered her mouth and immediately apologized. "I'm sorry, I don't know where that came from," she looked pleadingly at Sabine for help, but it was unnecessary as Cian came to her rescue.

"Put them down and join the others. Have a little respect the next time you enter a patient's room. Sebastian, bud, I'll be back later to talk about those ten minutes. Mara, find me if you need anything." He tossed Athena a cocky grin and then strode from the room, leaving them all staring after him.

Sabine sighed long and low. "I'm in love."

Athena huffed out a breath. "He's an ass."

"He's an ass you're going to have to suck up to if you want on his service," Sabine whispered as they followed Dr. Webster to the next patient room.

"Don't remind me."

chapter three

CIAN LET THE door to his penthouse apartment swing shut behind him and dropped his keys on the entryway table. It'd been a week since Henry Smalls had passed away unexpectedly on the table and he'd 'taken care of' the problem of Sally Pope. So far, there had been no suspicion over her death on the table; there never was when one of his special patients expired. His team was a well-oiled machine, each an integral part of making sure that their activities remained secret.

In the kitchen, he uncorked a bottle of fine red wine and poured himself a healthy glass. His chef had prepared salmon and steamed vegetables, leaving everything ready for him to heat and serve. With his hours at the hospital fluctuating as they did, there was little time for him to cook, no matter how much it was one of his favorite pastimes. His apartment showed off more of his style and little of his personality. Beige and cream paint colored the walls while modern art filled in the blank spaces. There were no splashes of color, no gaudy photo frames cluttering up his space. Everything was clean lines and open space. Neat and orderly just how he liked it.

Taking his warmed plate and glass of wine, he sat at his cream marble kitchen table and opened his portfolio to the section that held his notepad. A few clicks of a remote had his wall size flat-screen TV turning on to the local news station. He spent the next thirty minutes listening to the reports and pouring over the newspaper jotting down notes and information. One particular case on the news caught his attention and had him looking up.

"The young woman has been missing for three weeks now and frantic pleas from her parents for her safe return have gone viral in a heart breaking video posted on social media sites. Layla Hunt, eighteen, was last seen in New York City outside a theatre on 43rd Street. She was visiting the city with two girlfriends who have both given statements to the police. Foul play is suspected; a source tells us that this investigation has ties to the string of unsolved murders in the Louisiana a few months back. If you have any information that could lead to the safe return of Layla Hunt, please contact authorities immediately." Cian chewed his salmon thoughtfully as he recalled the details of the murdered women from a few months back. Apparently, the killer had a sick fetish for blood and got off on torturing the women for days before disposing of them. The trail had gone cold; that was until now when the killer had evidently resurfaced in New York City. He made several notes in his file to remind himself to do some digging. He'd never had a serial killer as one of his patients before but there was a first time for everything.

"—vigilante. *The Watcher* is what they're calling him. A man in the shadows that's protecting our city without us knowing about it." Cian's head snapped up and his eyes locked on the annoying, bubbly, former weather girl, Rae Kelley. She'd recently been appointed to a news anchor position and now every night at the city was treated—or tortured depending how you looked at it—to her presence on their screens relating the latest news.

"Criminals that have previously escaped persecution are conveniently ending up dead not long after they've been released from their charges. Is this a coincidence? Or does the city really have a protector watching over us and ridding us of criminals that have gotten away with unspeakable crimes? I'll be looking into these cases over the next few weeks and reporting on my online blog, *Rae's Ramblings*, so be sure to keep it locked on Channel 15 and bookmark my site."

Cian launched the remote across the room in disgust. How the hell had they picked up on the deaths not being accidental? And some dimwit weather reporter at that?

"Fuck." he swore. If they'd figured out that the criminals that skipped out on punishment were slowly going missing, and ultimately ending up dead, it was only a matter of time before their "investigation" lead them straight to him, and that was something he couldn't have. He'd have to speak to Reynolds about the OR notes and be sure that everything was iron-clad to show that the deaths on his table had been accidental and nothing more. His reputation would hold through some scrutiny but not something on a scale as large as this. He needed a plan and he needed it fast. The urge to kill was becoming stronger with every passing day and waiting the twenty-three days to take another victim was damn near killing him.

Feeling wound up, he rose from the table and dumped his dishes in the dishwasher. He needed release to get rid of the tension coiled inside him after watching that news broadcast. Walking into the living room, he grabbed his phone and scrolled through the numbers. None of the women jumped out at him and he fucking knew why. That intern with her unique, wide, olive-colored eyes was on his mind a hell of a lot more than she should be. Her stare had burned into him from the first second he'd seen her in the parking lot after he'd nearly mowed her down when she'd been standing stupidly in the middle of the road. Thinking she was some new nurse, he'd brushed her off, only to find her later at the bedside of one of his patients. Intelligence flashed in her eyes and he knew she was as sharp as they came. The fact that she'd held back when he knew she knew the answer pissed him off. To have knowledge and not use it was the highest form of idiocy and he wouldn't tolerate it, especially from someone that could end up assisting in his OR.

She had a bit of spunk in her though, he'd give her that. Her sassy comment to the asshole intern that had barged in the room like a bumbling buffoon had proven that. She would be a challenge and challenges were something that interested him. And if he was being honest with himself, the new little intern did interest him. He'd bet his life that smart mouth could be put to several good uses.

He changed clothes in his bedroom and then opened the door to a second bedroom that housed his home gym. A few hours working up a good sweat would push those eyes and that mouth out of his mind. The last thing he needed right now was the distraction of an unwanted woman, amazing eyes or not.

A coffee cup slid across the nurse's desk in front of Athena where she was charting vitals on the three patients she'd seen so far that shift. Glancing up, she smiled gratefully at Sabine who always seemed to know exactly what she needed. Their friendship was one of the things she treasured most in her life; she might drive her crazy with her insane ideas, but her fun-loving spirit was what made her who she was.

"Thanks. How's it going in the ER?" she asked. Webster had split them up that morning and Sabine had been one of the interns assigned to the ER for the day. It actually was one of the better assignments as the chances of being picked to observe in the OR were much higher than when rounding on patients and prescribing medications like she'd been doing all day.

"It's fucking unreal, Thene. You wouldn't believe the shit that's come through the door. A guy had a nail file in his eye. A nail file! His girlfriend shoved it there after finding pictures on his phone of him and another woman. But get this, it was his cousin, she just flipped out and wouldn't listen to the explanation! They were able to get it out without surgery though," her excited recounting ended with a frown, showing her disappointment at not being able to scrub in on the eye surgery.

Clarence and Oscar joined them, Clarence tossing an apple in the air and catching it before taking a bite. Oscar hung back a bit awkwardly, still not sure of his place in the group. It'd been two weeks since their first day and Athena had yet to hear him say more than five words unless he was speaking to Webster or a patient. Even Dick had warmed up slightly, although he was still a creep as far as Athena was concerned.

"Dude, I can't believe you're not more animated about this! We were in the OR, come on, crack a smile or something," Clarence said around a mouthful of apple.

"Wait, you were in the OR? Today? Like during a surgery?" Athena tried and failed to keep the jealously out of her tone.

"Damn right. Motor vehicle accident. Woman came in with multiple fractures and lacerations and some major damage to her abdomen. Smith was running the ER today and took us in with him. It was fucking awesome, Athena. You guys gotta get in on a surgery," Clarence was definitely riding the adrenaline of his first experience and although she wanted to remain envious, deep down she was happy for him. It gave her hope that not all the residents and attendings' thought they were wastes of space and would actually teach them. Oscar even cracked a grin and nodded to back up Clarence's story. Apparently the experience had even affected him.

"Not fucking fair. I was down there and Armstrong pulled out the damn nail file instead of going to surgery," Sabine complained, brushing Dick's arm away when he came up behind her and tugged on a lock of her hair. "Hands off, slimeball." Dick smirked and turned his attention to the group.

"You're looking at the first intern to be hand-picked to be at O'Reilly's side during his bypass surgery. Sorry, suckers, but you weren't here two hours before shift like I was to get in on that case." He drew in a breath through his nose as he hopped up onto the nurse's desk and looked down at all of them. "O'Reilly obviously is smart enough to know which one of us is the best intern in the class." Athena rolled her eyes and turned to walk away from the babbling idiot, only to collide with a hard chest.

"Oomph," she breathed out, almost losing her balance. Strong arms came up to steady her, encircling her waist. She had a second to breathe in the man's scent, as her nose was pushed up right against him, and it did funny things to her insides. He smelled clean, spicy and a little bit...dangerous? There was something about his scent that set off alarm bells in her head and longing in her pussy. Whoever it was that she'd nearly plowed over, he was a damn contradiction, that much was certain.

Chancing a look up, she was horrified to see it was Cian. He stood almost a foot taller than her at 6'4", why hadn't she noticed before how tall he was? His gaze was locked on hers and those dark eyes once again pulled her in, making her forget everything; including her own damn name. The man was a walking felony, it should be illegal for someone to look and smell as good as he did; especially considering he was such an asshole.

"Uh—I'm sorry," she apologized lamely, stepping back out of his arms. She looked around and flushed, noticing that their scene had caught more than one curious eye. Sabine was practically panting, encouraging her with her eyes to continue their display. She glared at her and looked back up at Cian.

"I didn't see you, Dr. O'Reilly. I'm sorry if I hurt you." Cian let out a chuckle that sounded rusty to her ears, but pleasant all the same.

"You barely come up to my shoulder, Dr. Payne. You didn't hurt me," he looked past her to Dick, pinning him in place with a hard glare. "So, you think you're the best in the program, do you? Tell me, what are you going to do if your patient develops a clot during surgery? Or begins to bleed profusely from the graft site? What's your approach going to be, doctor?" With each word he took a step closer to Dick until he was directly in front of him, an inch away from where Dick was beginning to cower. "Well? Are you going to sit there frozen like you are now and let your patient bleed to death? Is that what the best intern in this program would do?"

The hallway had gone deathly still as passerby's stopped to take in the scene. Dick's shoulders slumped and he rubbed the back of his neck frantically, his blue eyes darting back and forth.

"Yes. I mean, no. I mean, I would of course not let that happen, Dr. O'Reilly. I'd well, um..." he trailed off looking panicked, his mind clearly going blank under the pressure.

"You'd isolate the clot and call for a transfusion, examine the graft to see if it could be salvaged and if not, patch it up until another surgery could be booked to save the body any additional undue stress." Athena found herself speaking out of nowhere, something that was becoming a habit in Dr. O'Reilly's presence.

Cian's head swiveled slowly towards her and he regarded her with approval. Her heart was pounding so hard in her chest it felt like a set of drums were banging behind her ears. Had she really just blurted out the answer like that? Sure, surgery was a cutthroat profession and it was every man for themselves, but had she really just made a fool of one of her own in front of everyone? It appeared she had as the glances she was receiving were a cross between respect and resentment.

She shifted from foot to foot and twirled the diamond stud earring at her ear in an effort to calm her nerves. They were her favorite pair, a gift from her father on the last birthday he'd been alive. A prized possession of hers, she never took them off, wearing them daily felt as though she carried a piece of him everywhere she went.

"You're in." Cian pointed at her. "You, you're out. Go find your brains and some balls and then we'll talk about you "assisting" in my OR. I catch you shooting your mouth off like that again and I'll make sure the only sharp object you touch this century is a No.2 pencil." He finished his chastising of Dick just as Bianca and Webster joined them; Bianca's arms weighed down with charts.

"Surgery in ten minutes. Get scrubbed," he ordered Athena as he passed. She didn't miss the subtle brush of his arm against hers, although she fought like hell to suppress the spark of electricity it sent tingling down her spine.

Sabine barged over and grabbing her by the upper arm, dragged her to the waiting area. "Oh, my God! Thene!" she squealed. "First, I fucking hate that you're getting in the OR before me. Second, you little whore, you totally want a piece of him!"

"Shhhhh, oh, my God, would you shut up? I do not want a piece of him," she hissed back, face on fire.

"You do. I saw the chemistry, the connection. Jesus Murphy, it's like the rest of us in this hospital ceased to exist when you two were staring into each other's eyes," she batted her eyelashes for effect.

"Shut up. I banged into him that's all and had to apologize. Then that idiot, Dick couldn't answer a simple question and I seized an opportunity. I didn't mean to make him look foolish, but if I want to get in on these cardiac surgeries, I have to jump when opportunity knocks." Athena tried to justify her actions not only to Sabine, but to herself. Covering her face with her hands, she sighed.

"It was epic. I love that being here is starting to bring out the badass side of you that I always knew was hiding in there." Sabine pulled her hands away and steered her towards the elevators. "Now go. This is no damn nail file case, this is your first time in a surgery, Thene! Go get some action," she winked at her making sure she caught her double meaning before the elevators doors separated them. Athena stood staring at her own reflection in the stainless steel doors, pulse racing and skin tingling in anticipation.

"I'm so screwed."

chapter four

THERE'S A SWEET spot of time in the hospital when all is quiet and peaceful. You never know what time of day its going to happen, but when it does, it's as though the whole place recognizes that a few minutes of serenity are needed to keep things flowing. Patients rest more comfortably, bickering among co-workers is silenced, phones and pagers cease beeping and letting out shrill rings. It's the sweet spot and when you're in it, nothing can touch you; not even death. Cian had never paid attention to the rumblings about that particular superstition, but over the past month since the new crop of interns integrated his hospital, he'd found himself buying into it more and more. And the reason was very simple—Athena Payne. Her innocence, her optimism was starting to affect him in a way that was unsettling. Now on the eve of the twenty-third day, he found himself more distracted with thoughts of her than focused on the patient they were bringing in that night.

She was quickly becoming a star in her own right. Every attending requested her on their service and Webster and Murphy couldn't shut up about her. Her disastrous start was long forgotten and instead the bright, shining career she was going to have as a surgeon was all anyone talked about. Even her co-workers looked at her with admiration as opposed to envy, which was a feat in itself. Except for that dumbass, Dick. That douche gave her a hard time every chance he could, but Athena seemed to take it all in stride.

He finished closing up his patient, and peeled off his gloves as he exited the OR to scrub out. His mind drifted back to the first time she'd stepped into his OR, the same day they'd crashed into each other and he'd got a feel of that lush little body of hers. Her breasts had been smashed into his chest and the top of her head had been at the perfect height for him to inhale the scent of her fragrant hair. Something had passed between them that day in those few moments she was in his arms; he knew she felt it too.

When she'd stepped into the OR a short while later, gowned, gloved and scrubbed, it felt right. As though she belonged as a part of his team. He didn't allow her to touch any instruments that day—she was still an intern after all—but he was still impressed with the way her intelligent eyes tracked not only his every move, but every move of the the nurses, residents, and other doctors involved in the surgery. A good surgeon knew how to anticipate, who to rely on and what each of their team member's strengths were. With the way Athena absorbed every tiny detail in that room, he knew she would be a pro at that particular part of the game in no time.

Her confidence might not have been the highest, but she was starting to come out of her shell. She observed the procedure with a watchful eye and answered every question he threw at her, even ones beyond a first year intern's comprehension. When they'd finished, he caught up with her in the scrub room.

"You did well. I hit you with some tough questions," he commented.

"I've been studying and reading, tracking down research articles on all of your cases. I want to learn; be prepared." she answered without looking up.

"My cases? I assume you have an interest in cardiothoracic surgery then."

"Yes. It's what I want to specialize in, I've dreamed about this chance for years." A slow grin formed on her face and lit up her eyes. "I know this is going to sound unprofessional, but God, I loved it in there! The rush, the adrenaline, the feeling of power pumping around the room. I may have just stood there but I was actually in a surgery. With you—Dr. O'Reilly. I can't tell you what this means to me. Thank you," her voice was filled with sincerity and she was looking at him with such awe. Innocence such as hers didn't have any place around someone like him. The depraved soul that lived beneath the exterior he showed the outside world would devour her in seconds, feeding on her purity until she was destroyed. And worst of all, he'd find pleasure in every second of it.

Shaking himself back to the present, he paged Reynolds to the attendings' lounge. Grabbing a quick cup of coffee while he waited, he debated whether he had time to coax one of the Pediatric nurses into an on-call room to help him relieve some of the stress that had him wound up. Before he could make a decision one way or another, the door opened and Reynolds entered, looking frazzled.

"Sorry, Cian. It's been a bad luck shift. Lost two on the table." He made his way over to the coffee pot and poured himself a cup. "Fuck, I wish this was scotch."

"Is everything set? I'm ready to leave now to get the package." Cian cut right to the chase, eager to get started. He needed this, to hunt, to kill. The desire was starting to unfold in him; working its way up from his toes until it consumed every inch of him. His skin was singing in anticipation as he relished the thought of what was to come. This man, this piece of scum they'd marked for death had no idea what was coming for him.

"We're set. See you in the OR in thirty." Reynolds knew Cian well enough that when he slipped on the mask of his alter-ego, there was no talking to him. He became something else; something sinister and dark. His rage was a living part of his soul that he didn't bother to harness. Instead, nurturing it and letting it flourish into what he was now. A cold-blooded killer. God help anyone that ever got on his bad side.

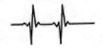

Cian circled the warehouse once before rolling his car to a stop and killing the lights. The second shift break was about to finish at the distribution center and from his surveillance, he knew Darwin Fergus would be slinking out the side door to sneak in an extra smoke break before heading back to work. He got out of the car and crouched down behind a dumpster a few feet away from where he was sure Darwin would be exiting the building, remaining unseen until the opportunity he needed presented itself. Keeping an eye out for anyone that might spot him, he thought back over the information he'd gathered on him while he waited for his target to appear.

Darwin Fergus, age 42
Arrested on multiple counts of fraud, larceny, and suspected homicide
Released after insufficient evidence brought to the DA to hold the case over to trial
Estimated net worth stolen over $200,000 over the past ten years. *Victims of choice:*
elderly and disabled

So the fucker liked to take advantage of old people with his schemes and lies, ultimately swindling them out of their retirement checks. He'd crippled dozens of individuals financially and in some cases, it was suspected he'd caused their deaths by overdoses on medications when he was close to being exposed. The only reason he'd been arrested was in thanks to one of the victim's grandchildren overhearing part of a conversation and putting the pieces together. Unfortunately, it wasn't soon enough and her grandfather had been one of the ones to lose his life. She'd come forward with what she knew, but it wasn't enough to convict and he'd walked away a free man. *Until now.*

Like clockwork, the side door opened and Darwin slipped out. Cian slipped the needle from his pocket and with the stealth of a predator, approached him from behind and pounced, locking an arm around his neck and cutting off his air supply. Darwin was not a small man by any means and outweighed him by almost fifty pounds. But where Darwin was large and soft, Cian was lean and hard. His strength won out and he had Darwin down on the ground and the needle inserted in his neck before he could even muster a shout.

"Fuck, you're heavy," he complained, panting hard as he looked down at the disgusting excuse for a man at his feet. Taking him by the ankles, he made short work of dragging him to his waiting open trunk. It would be a tight fit, but he'd made it work before and he'd do so again. The interior was lined with plastic, ready and waiting to transport the fucker to the hospital. Grunting from the exertion, he wrestled Darwin into the trunk and slammed it, satisfied.

"Let's go for a ride, shall we?" He got no reply, not that he expected one, and hopped in the driver's seat. About a block from the hospital he pulled into an alleyway and stopped. Dragging Darwin from the trunk, he smacked him in the face until he came around, groaning from being groggy and out of it.

"Are you with me there, Darwin? Can you hear me?" Cian peered at him, his pupils were dilated but he seemed to be understanding him.

"Ghaft ahappped?" his words were a gargled mess. Good. The drugs were working.

"Oh, not to worry. I'm gonna take good care of you, Darwin." Relief flashed in his eyes but it quickly turned to horror as he watched Cian pick up an iron bar from the trunk. "Don't worry, you won't feel a thing," his grin was full of malice as he brought the bar down.

Several minutes later, Cian rushed into the ER, with Darwin's arms over his shoulders, dragging him along as best he could.

"Get me a gurney! This man's taken a severe beating," he helped two orderlies lift Darwin onto the gurney when they raced over. He tossed his keys to Jenson who was standing a few feet away, wide-eyed. "My car is in an alley a block away. Get it and move it here. Do not fuck that up, Jenson," he ordered. Jenson nodded and hurried away to follow instructions.

Reynolds appeared in the hallway and after a slight nod, Cian called out to the nurse behind the desk.

"Book me OR-B, I'm heading up there now with him. His injuries are extreme and we need to get in there now." The nurse nodded and grabbed for the phone, barking orders that the OR was needed stat.

Following behind the gurney, Cian's steps were filled with glee. Another successful hunt and soon it would be another successful kill and scumbag eliminated. He should get a goddamn fucking medal for the clean-up work he did for the city. Vigilante his ass, he was a motherfucking saint.

"Oh!" He whipped his head around at the sound of a startled squeal and locked eyes with Athena who was standing directly in front of him with an armload of charts and a fresh green salad. She took in his appearance slowly, the blood staining his clothes and the manic look in his eyes. Confusion and then fear flashed across her features as she tried to make sense of what she was seeing.

She took a small step forward, but Cian cut her off before she could speak. "Out of the way, Dr. Payne. Can't you see we have a critical patient here?" he barked, watching her flinch at his tone. Flustered, she stepped back quickly.

"I—I'm sorry. I thought..." she stammered.

"You thought what? You thought whatever you needed to say was more important than this man getting to surgery? I'd pegged you for smarter than that," he stepped around her without another word and ignored the twinge of guilt he felt at seeing the hurt in her eyes his words caused. It was for the best that she stop idolizing him in more than a mentor capacity. Nothing would ever come of the connection between them. It was ridiculous to think otherwise.

He headed into the scrub room to prepare while the team got Darwin prepped for surgery. A black rage had settled over him, more intense than he'd ever felt before. The fear he'd seen in Athena's eyes haunted him. *Was she afraid of him?* She was right to be, but he'd never hurt her. The fact that she might think he would, bothered him more than he liked, turning his anger into a murderous rage.

Entering the OR, he stalked straight to Darwin's side, satisfied when he saw that he was coherent. "Mr. Fergus, good evening. Pleasure to have you here in my OR." Darwin struggled against the binds holding down his arms and legs, eyes frozen in fear as Reynolds' approached from the other side and fitted him with the gag.

"Sorry, guess we won't be hearing much more from you, now will we? What a shame. I was looking forward to hearing all about how you weaseled money away from the elderly; how you murdered the ones that were close to figuring out your con. You're despicable, you know that? To rob the elderly is like harming defenseless babies. Did it make you feel powerful? Did you enjoy the thrill of taking from another? Did you get off on it, Darwin?" The more he spoke, the closer he got until they were almost nose to nose. Darwin's entire body was quaking in fear; fear that Cian fed off, his terror transported into his blood and gave him the initiative he craved to get the job done.

"Saw," he demanded. Patricia complied and handed him the small bone saw. Fixing on his goggles, he cheerfully got to work, starting with Darwin's right index finger. He lowered the blade and applied just the right amount of pressure to torturously cut through the skin and bone, removing the finger completely. Darwin's body bucked and thrashed and he screamed with all his might into the gag, but none of that halted Cian's task. He removed two more fingers before tiring of the saw and switching tactics.

"Do you know, losing all your money...it's like dying a slow death. First, they take your electricity. Then, you have no money for food. Not long after that, they'll repossess your belongings. Until finally, they take your home from you. Have you ever been homeless, Darwin? Ever lost everything that meant something to you? It's agonizing. And you—you caused that for these people. They trusted you and you took advantage, ruining what little of their lives they had left. And when they didn't comply? Well, then you stole their lives. I think it's only fair you feel some agony as well. Scalpel."

Lorna passed him the scalpel and he expertly made a small incision in Darwin's neck, pleasure filling him as he watched the blood seep from the wound and onto the table. Darwin gurgled and choked, his own blood starting to strangle him.

Cian leaned down to whisper in his ear. "I could leave you like this for hours. You'd bleed out, or you'd maybe strangle on your blood first, who knows. What matters to me is that you suffer."

Darwin's eyes pleaded with him for mercy, begged for forgiveness, screamed to be released. None of it mattered, his fate was sealed. He had another flash of Athena's terrified face and the rage increased tenfold. Grabbing the scalpel again, he brutally slashed down Darwin's midsection, determined to rid himself of the vision of Athena.

"O'Reilly," Reynolds warned. "Get a grip, we've got five minutes. Finish it."

Panting, Cian took a breath and looked around. His team's faces held expressions of shock, not something he was used to after everything they'd witnessed him do. He was losing it; needed to get a grip as Reynolds said.

"I'm fine. I got this." Shaking his head, he used incision he'd made in Darwin's midsection to properly open him up. After a few minutes of "repairing" damage to the kidneys and large intestine, he made the cut that would end Darwin's life. He watched as the life drained from his glazed-over eyes, filled with a sick satisfaction that left him feeling more on top of his game than ever.

"Good work, team. Clean up and I'll take care of the notes this time." He left his team staring after him, wondering if the man they followed so blindly was starting to slip off his game or descend too far into the hell he'd created to ever find a way back.

chapter five

"**T**HE CITY IS starting to panic as yet another young woman has gone missing, assumed taken at the hands of the same suspect that's presumed to have Layla Hunt, the eighteen-year-old girl from Louisiana. This morning, Cheryl Fuller reported her daughter, Candice missing. Candice was last seen in Times Square with a large group of friends. Police are actively investigating and urge any witnesses with information on either young women, to please come forward." Cian looked up as a photo splashed across the screen of a young brunette in a cheerleader's uniform.

He was catching a bit of down time in the attendings' lounge before his next surgery. It had been one hell of a day already with two emergency surgeries on top of his regular cases. Dragging a hand through his dark hair he sighed and turned his attention back to the news station just as Rae Kelley came on screen. Her blonde hair was piled on her head in some bun-type thing and her breasts all but spilled out of the black dress she wore as she bounced her step on her blood-red high heels. Cian rolled his eyes at her image, how she got that job was beyond him.

"Good evening, ladies and gentlemen," she began before pausing and staring at something off in the distance. "Oh! Good afternoon, I mean...good afternoon, ladies and gentlemen." Her face burned red from her on-air mistake and Cian having no patience for idiocy, was about to switch her off when her next words caught his attention.

"We have an update on *The Watcher*, the vigilante who we believe has been eliminating criminals who have escaped justice in the legal system. Sources tell us that one, Darwin Fergus, who died just over two weeks ago, was in fact a victim of our unknown protector. If you'll recall, Fergus was accused of running a fraudulent con-artist scheme that cheated several dozens of elderly people out of their retirement funds. There were also allegations raised that a few suspicious deaths may have been at his hand in an attempt to cover up what he'd done. With not enough evidence to prosecute, he was let go much to the outrage of the community.

After a back alley beating, he died from complications during surgery. Coincidence? Or is this again the work of *The Watcher*? We'll keep you updated as information regarding this comes available, don't forget to tune in to Channel 15 and check out my blog, *Rae's Ramblings*."

Furious, Cian shoved himself up from the leather sofa and paced around the room like a caged cat. That fucking nosey idiot reporter was getting way to close to finding out the truth. And who the hell were these "sources" she claimed she got her information from? Everyone on his team had as much at stake as he did and he knew without a doubt he could trust each of them. But did he really? The only people that knew the truth were the six people on his team. Perhaps it was time he started looking for a mole.

In the hallway, he ran into Reynolds who was just finishing up a conversation with the Chief. "Reynolds, Chief," he greeted them as he walked up.

Chief Murphy clasped him on the shoulder and steered him aside. "Damn good work getting those two transplant cases into our hospital, O'Reilly. The media attention is just what this place needs and that kind of initiative is what sets you apart from the rest. Keep it up and you just might be a good candidate for my position one day."

"Well, sir, I can't say that wouldn't please me, although I know we're several years off from that happening. Still, thank you for the recognition. I have a few other high profile cases to discuss with you as well that I'd like to bring in."

Murphy grinned and nodded. "Call my secretary and have her set up a time for this week. I want to hear more about this."

Telling him he'd do that, Cian glanced to the left and watched as Webster came into the main foyer with her six interns trailing behind her. Each had their heads hung as though in shame and from the way Webster's head was tossing and her hip was cocked, he guessed they were getting in shit. The guilty expressions confirmed it, all except Athena. She didn't look guilty or remorseful; she looked pissed. Curious, he moved closer to find out what the issue was.

"—interns. You have no business making a diagnosis and you most certainly have no business telling a patient they have an incurable brain tumor! What in the bloody hell is the matter with you?" Webster was livid, her voice raising with each word she spit out. "I want to know right now who it was that spoke to Mr. Seymour about his wife." They kept silent, looking at the floor or ceiling, refusing to meet Webster's furious glare. Except Athena, she stared at her head on, barely even blinking. Cian knew immediately what she was going to do.

"It was me. I told Mr. Seymour about the tumor, Dr. Webster." Athena admitted, shocking everyone.

"Payne? Why would you do such a thing? Do you understand now that I have to go and explain to those poor people that they *don't* have to worry about terminal cancer? What were you thinking? Is that the kind of patient care you want to give as a doctor?"

Athena was quiet for a moment, unsure of how to answer. She wasn't the one that screwed up, it was Dick, but seeing how he clearly wasn't going to man up, someone had to or they'd never find their way out of the mess. To make matters worse, Cian was hovering behind Webster, witnessing her humiliation as she took the fall for something she didn't do.

"No, Dr. Webster, that's not how I want to care for my patients. I honestly thought I was doing the right thing." There, that wasn't a total lie.

"I thought you were smarter than this, Payne. I really did. I'm disappointed in you."

"Ahem," Cian stepped forward and cleared his throat. He had no idea what he was doing. He'd avoided all contact with Athena since the night they'd run into each other with Fergus. Now here he was getting in the middle of something that didn't concern him. Still, he couldn't stop himself.

"Dr. Webster, if I may. Isn't the point of being an intern that you're going to make mistakes? We rely on those mistakes to teach us what not to do in the future. I think I remember a time or two that you were in some hot water with your resident." He raised an eyebrow at her and watched as she paled at the memory of her own transgressions. "Athena is one of our strongest interns, perhaps maybe look a little beneath the surface and see what really happened here before believing everything you're told." With that, he turned on his heel and walked away, still shocked that he'd risen to the defense of a female, an intern no less in front of half the hospital. He didn't have to glance back to feel all the eyes boring into his back or hear the tongues start wagging with gossip. *Great. Just fucking great.*

Faye Webster was one of the most respected residents in the Lincoln Hospital surgical program. To receive a dressing down in front of her colleagues and subordinates was not something she ever expected to have happen to her. The need to lash out was fierce, but she kept her cool and turned skeptical eyes to Athena.

"Payne, are you covering for someone?" The insinuation made by O'Reilly that she was missing information was not lost on her. Her instincts might have been right after all when she was completely blown away by Payne's confession.

Backed into a corner, Athena didn't know what to do or say. If she lied again now, and was found out later it would come back on her worse. But if she told the truth, she'd be throwing Dick under the bus. At a loss, she glared hard at Dick, willing him to come forward on his own. He of course, stared back defiantly, refusing to budge. Left with no choice, she did the only thing she could.

"Yes. But don't ask me who. We all have to work together as a team, you've told us that from the beginning. If we can't rely on each other to have each other's backs outside of the OR, how are we ever going to learn to work together to save lives in the OR?" Her question was met with silence while Faye stared at her, considering her words. Finally, she sighed.

"Fine. But all of you will be present while I explain this situation to the family. If I have to suffer through it, so do you."

Sabine fell back into step with Athena as they headed to speak to the family. "Oh, my fucking God, Thene!" she hissed. "He came to your rescue, he spoke up in front of everyone for you! He so wants in your panties. He wants those panties off you bad. Dude, he wants you to never be wearing panties when he's around!"

"Shhh, shut up! Enough about my panties. And he wasn't defending me, he was helping. Helping avoid a scene," she finished lamely, clueless on what to say. The truth was, she had no idea why Cian interjected the way he did. For the past several weeks, since that night she'd run into him on his way to the OR, she'd done her best to avoid him. Something about him that night was different; he was different. She could see it in his eyes. The feral way he'd bared his teeth and snapped at her had sent terror skidding down her spine and she barely restrained herself from sprinting at a dead run away from him. But as much as she was scared, she was also intrigued. There was a conflicted war happening inside her where Cian O'Reilly was concerned. A war she was petrified she was going to lose. Especially if he kept up riding in like some white knight in shining armor. Although in his case, it was more like a dark avenging angel.

"Ugh, you can be so blind sometimes! Mark my words, Athena, it won't be long before instead of him riding in like your white knight—" Athena's head whipped up when Sabine plucked the thoughts right out of her head. "—he's got you riding him instead."

Athena smacked her on the arm and blushed furiously as the image of sliding herself down onto Cian's waiting cock filled her head. He'd reach up and tug her long hair back, exposing her throat to his teeth; biting down and marking her flesh as his as he slowly entered her, rocking his hips up and into her in a way that would have her moaning out his name. She'd start to move in a leisurely pace at first and then—

"You're totally picturing it! You have sex face!" Sabine exclaimed far too loudly. The entire group turned to gape at the two of them and Athena wished furiously for the floor to open up and swallow her, or better yet, to swallow her asshole best friend.

She caught a look of hurt flash across Clarence's face but before she could wonder what that was about, Bianca burst out laughing, breaking the silence.

"You two are a trip," she commented, shaking her head in disbelief. Webster glared at all of them and motioned them into the room with her hands.

"God save me from interns," she muttered, closing the door behind them.

Reynolds stopped him in the hall on his way out of the building a few hours after his run in with Webster and her interns. The gossips had already been churning over his latest stunt and rumors were running rampant about a torrid affair between him and the little Dr. Payne.

"Have you seen the news lately?" Reynolds asked, concern evident in his tone.

"Yeah. It's a goddamn nightmare. Where the hell is that nitwit getting her info?"

"I don't know. I was hoping you had some idea. What's our plan of action here? Are we cooling things off for awhile until this blows over?" Reynolds asked.

"Fuck no. Are you crazy? We can't stop now. These fuckers need to pay for what they've done, Reynolds. I thought you understood that." Cian snapped.

"Calm down. Of course I understand that, but neither of us need this shit coming down on our heads," he lowered his voice. "We're murdering people, Cian. Right here in this hospital under the fucking nose of everyone. And someone knows about it and is feeding information to the press. Doesn't that concern you even a little?"

"You're damn right it concerns me. It concerns me enough to know we need to find the mole and flush this shit out now. Someone is talking, you're right about that, and when I catch who it is, they're going to wish they never crossed me. That's a promise." They headed out the sliding doors and into the dusky light of the just setting sun.

"Well if you won't consider giving it a rest for awhile then we need to be really fucking careful on the twenty-third. It's only a couple weeks away and I don't want to have the cops showing up in our OR."

"That's not going to happen. I'm going to handle this spy or mole or whatever the fuck it is and you're going to help me. Set up a meet of the team at my place tomorrow. I want everyone there, no excuses."

"Alright. Cian, are you sure there isn't anything I can say to change your mind about taking a break for awhile? I really think—"

"No. How can you even say that to me, John? You know the significance of that date. You know why we have to keep moving forward with this. If you want off the team, fine. But just fucking say that instead of acting like a pussy and wanting a break. We're not fucking dating." Cian's temper snapped and he took a few menacing steps forward into Reynolds' space. It wasn't often he called him by his first name, but the slight slip showed just how close he was to losing control.

"You're right, I'm sorry. No, I don't want off the team, I still believe in what we're doing. I just want this fucking shit put to bed."

Cian stared at him hard for a few long moments before walking to his car and wrenching open the door. He leaned over the top of it and the look in his eyes was chilling as he spoke.

"Fine. But don't push me on this again. I guarantee you won't like the side of me it brings out."

chapter six

CIAN LEFT THE hospital and drove towards home, the genius idea of stopping off to pick up some fresh daisies to surprise his beautiful wife, Hannah, with popping in his head. The local floral shop would be pleased with the business and he'd be blessed with one of Hannah's "special" smiles as she called them, the dazzling one she saved for just the right moments, and hopefully a mind-blowing marathon of sex later that night in bed.

Their anniversary was coming up in a few months, five years of marriage. Quite an accomplishment in this day and age. He had plans to surprise her with a romantic cruise around the Caribbean, he just had a few more details to work out in his schedule at work and then he'd be making the reservations. She'd argue with him over the money of course, they were complete opposites in that sense, she was frugal and seriously contemplated over every penny they spent, while he didn't give a shit about what things cost. They brought in a more than decent living between his salary at the hospital and hers as the Assistant District Attorney.

With demanding careers, their schedules didn't allow for a lot of down time for the luxury of things like vacations, so pulling this off was going to be a huge feat on his part. Luckily, Hannah had an amazing assistant that was helping to clear her schedule in a subtle way so that the cruise would be a surprise. He couldn't wait to see her reaction.

Pulling into the driveway of their home in the suburbs of New York, he glanced at Hannah's old beat up Toyota Corolla and grimaced. He really needed to put his foot down and talk her into letting them purchase her a better vehicle. A nice SUV, something that he wouldn't worry the wheels would fall off of as she drove down the road. Ever since he'd met her, she'd been stubborn and strong-willed, yet with a heart of gold. Her compassion for others and her drive and ambition were the main things that attracted him to her.

The first time he'd seen her in line at a concession stand at a New York Rangers game, he'd thought she was adorable; all decked out in her Boston Bruins gear. Damn ballsy of her at a Rangers game, but as he learned over the next several months, she was spirited and had no problem standing up and cheering for her team at an away game. Her laugh and smile were so infectious at that first game that he had no choice but to charm his way into a date with her, beers at a local pub after the game to celebrate the Bruins win. Since then, it'd been history. They married six months later in a small ceremony of mostly her friends and family since Cian didn't have a large amount of either, and had been living their dream together ever since.

Sliding the key into the lock, he opened the door and stepped into their home. It was a modest house, three bedrooms and three bathrooms. On the large side for just the two of them but they were hoping to try and start a family at some point over the next couple of years. Timing seemed to always get in their way with both of their busy professions.

"Hannah? Babe? Where are you?" It was strange that she wasn't puttering about in the kitchen fixing their dinner. They both loved to cook and alternated on making meals depending on who got home first. Since this was his heavier week at work, she'd been handling most of the cooking all week.

Confused at the silence that met him, he set the bouquet of flowers down on the counter and wandered into the living room. Finding nowhere there, he headed upstairs. The house was eerily quiet, but he brushed it off thinking it was his imagination after a long shift at the hospital. Thinking she might have wanted a nice hot bath after a long day herself, he opened the door to their bedroom.

"Babe? Are you—" he broke off at the sight before him and letting out a roar, rushed into the room. Hannah was sitting straight up on their bed, hands and feet bound and mouth gagged, tears streaming down her face as she tried to scream from behind the sock stuffed in her mouth. Enraged, he charged towards her not noticing the frantic shaking of her head.

A searing pain in the back of his head had him crashing to the floor as he was hit with a metal object from behind. Hannah cried harder and her muffled screams got louder as Cian rolled to his side with a groan. Looking up, he had a split second to shuffle across the floor out of the way as their assailant brought the crow bar down again, missing him by inches. He managed to get to his knees and tackle the other man to the floor where they rolled over the carpet in a flurry of legs and fists. He got a few good hits in but the attacker outweighed him by at least one hundred pounds and hit like a sledgehammer. He took a blow to the nose that had him crashing onto his back and seeing stars.

When he was finally able to sit up, he froze. The man was standing with a gun to Hannah's head, staring hard at him. The fact that his face wasn't covered told him that it was no normal robbery and that had Cian scared shitless.

"Okay, now just hold on." He tried to gain his feet and grimaced when his head spun. That damn hit really did a number on him. "Just put that down and tell me what you want. Anything you want is yours. You want money? Name your price. Just please, don't hurt my wife."

"Anything I want? You can bring my brother back from the dead? You got that kind of power, huh, tough guy?" He jammed the barrel of the gun hard into Hannah's temple, ignoring her whimper of pain.

Cian inched forward again and the man cocked the gun. "You want to stay right there, tough guy and don't fucking move or I swear to God you're going to be wearing her brains."

Swallowing hard, Cian held up his hands. "I'm not moving, I'm co-operating. You're in charge here, I understand that. I'm sorry about your brother, really I am, but I don't know how to fix that for you."

"Ain't no fucking fixin' it! It's her fucking fault!" He grabbed Hannah by the hair and dragged her over to his side of the bed. "Your fucking cunt of a wife sent him to prison and they fucking killed him in there. Knifed him over and over like he was a damn pig. He was my brother; he didn't deserve to go out like that!"

Hannah's eyes met Cian's and she pleaded with him to help her, the terror she was feeling written all over her face. Feeling powerless, he wanted to lash out so bad he could taste it. To rip her away from him and tuck her into his side where she would be safe.

"I'm sorry. I really am sorry about your brother, but the blame belongs on the person that killed him in prison, not on us. They are the ones you should be angry with, not my wife. She would never have wanted anything to happen to him; look tell me...what was his name? I bet she will remember the case if you tell us his name—she remembers every single case."

The attacker looked skeptical for a moment but then his facial features smoothed out and his dark green eyes lost a bit of their edge of rage. "His name was Roy Combs. He was only twenty-one."

Cian looked at Hannah and she nodded slightly, indicating that she remembered the case. "Mr. Combs, my wife remembers your brother, please let her tell you what she knows, take the gag off and talk to her. Just the gag, that's all I'm asking." Combs hesitated for a few minutes, the room growing more thick with tension if that was possible, but he gave in and he removed the gag from Hannah's mouth.

"I'm sorry, I'm sorry, babe," she burst out, looking at Cian. "I love you so much, I didn't know, I answered the door and ah—" she cried out when Combs savagely ripped her head back by the hair.

"Shut the fuck up, bitch. You think I took that out so you could talk to him? No. You fucking tell me what you know about my brother right the fuck now." Combs shoved the gun under her eyes, ignoring the way she squirmed and cried.

"Hannah, babe. Look at me. It's going to be okay, I promise. Just look at me, and tell him what you remember about the case, babe." Not being able to be by her side was fucking ripping Cian's heart out. He needed to get him distracted long enough so that he could make a move and get her the hell out of there.

"R—Roy was a g—good kid. He got in some trouble with the wrong crowd and took the fall for something he didn't do. I t— tried to get through to him, to get him to tell me who the real culprit was, but he was s—scared. He took the sentence as a show of good faith to the crew he was running with. I h—heard after, they put the hit on him not believing that he would keep his mouth shut." Hannah dragged her gaze away from Cian and looked at Combs. "He was a good kid, your brother."

Combs let a single tear escape and nodded his head once. "Yeah. Yeah he was a good kid."

A small flutter of relief washed over Cian as he saw they'd finally gotten through to Combs. All he'd needed was the truth and to know that someone cared about his kid brother. It wasn't so hard to understand in the grand scheme of things. Now all he had to do was—

"You fucking knew. You fucking knew he was innocent and you let him go in there anyways. It is your fucking fault! Your fucking fault!" Combs screamed, waving the gun around. Cian rushed forward and grabbed Hannah, dragging her off the bed and shoving her down on the floor. Furious, Combs charged forward swinging out. Cian ducked and avoid the punch but not the tackle to the midsection and they ended up on the floor again. He could see Hannah out of the corner of his eye frantically trying to get her feet untied. Once she succeeded, he rolled over on top of Combs with all his might and started raining down punches.

"Run! Run, Hannah!" he ordered her, relieved that for once she wasn't stubborn and listened to him. Combs got his bearings back and rolled them back over starting to climb to his feet to chase her. Cian's hand shot out and pulling his ankle was able to slow him down enough for her to make it out of the room. Seconds later he heard her scream and scrambled to his feet wondering what the fuck had happened now.

He didn't have long to wait to find out as she was dragged back into the room by another man, a shorter, stockier man who also had a gun.

"'Bout fucking time you showed up. Get that bitch back in here," Combs ordered, grabbing Cian's arms and twisting them behind his back. The second attacker complied, dragging a struggling Hannah back into the room.

"Oh yeah, baby, keep wiggling that ass against me, I fucking love it." His free hand cupped her breast roughly as he ground his hips into her. "You're a fucking real wild one aren't ya? Bet you're a dynamite fuck."

"Get your fucking hands off my wife!" Cian roared. He managed to drag both him and Combs two steps before stars exploded behind his eyes once again and he crashed to the floor. His vision swam and he barely felt the third blow of the crow bar come down across his head. He got a brief glance at Hannah and thought he heard her scream out, "Cian, I love you!" before there was a loud bang and everything went black.

When he next opened his eyes, pain was his first realization. Every molecule of his body was on fire. An inferno of agony. He tried to lift his hand and noticed there was a long white tube attached to it. He recognized the ceiling of his bedroom and could see the feet of several different people as they moved around his room. Sitting up, he blinked.

"H—Hannah," he croaked, his voice dry and rusty. The female paramedic that was currently injecting something into the IV in his arm, set her mouth in a grim line and didn't answer him. "Where is she?" he demanded, pushing more steel into his voice.

"Mr. O'Reilly, you've suffered some major trauma to your head and we really need you to just lie still for now."

"Where the fuck is she?" he yelled, losing all patience. Dread was starting to coil in his belly. He replayed the last few moments before he passed out. The second assailant coming in, being hit from behind once more, the loud bang...

"Oh, God, no. Please no." Frantically his eyes scanned the room until they landed on a still form in the corner of the room covered with a white sheet.

"NO!" he screamed, shoving to his feet, knocking the paramedic over as he raced to fall to his knees beside the body. "Hannah, please no. Please, please babe, no." He pulled the sheet back and the agonized scream that wrenched from his body at the sight of his wife lying dead on their bedroom floor broke every heart in the room. Gathering her in his arms, he buried his face in her hair and let the tears fall, not caring who heard or saw him. His wife, his beautiful, perfect wife. Dead. And it was all his fault.

"I love you, I love you. I love you, Hannah. Fuck, no. Please no, baby. Don't leave me," he whispered into her hair, rocking her body back and forth.

"Mr. O'Reilly. Mr. O'Reilly, we really need to get you to the hospital to be looked at. That gash on your head is serious. The police need to—"

"Get the fuck out. I'm a doctor. I'm a fucking doctor. Just get out and leave us alone." Deciding to give him a bit of time alone but still keep an eye on him, they backed off and left him to grieve in silence with his wife.

Several hours later, he finally let them take her from him and in a daze was loaded in the ambulance and transferred to the hospital. The next few weeks were a blur as he underwent a minor cosmetic surgery to repair the damage to his skull and went through the motions of planning a funeral service. When John Reynolds found him standing alone at Hannah's grave in the pitch black of night on the day of her burial, he did his best to coax him to come and stay with him for a few days.

"Cian, please. We just want to help you. Tell me what we can do."

He raised his eyes to his long-time friend, eyes that were vacant of any emotion. Looking back at the gravestone he mumbled a few words that Reynolds didn't catch.

"What? I didn't hear you. What did you say?"

"May 23rd," he voiced the day Hannah had died. Reynolds had a fleeting moment where he truly thought Cian had lost his mind.

"May 23rd," he repeated and then pinned John with a glare so fierce it nearly burned right through him. "You want to help, John? Fine. I have a plan."

May 23rd. The day that the last good part of him died and the monster within was born; ready to seek vengeance for all that he'd lost.

chapter seven

Present Day

LIFE AS AN intern at Lincoln Hospital was starting to become more of a routine for Athena. Each day brought in new cases and opportunities to end up in surgery. The six of them assigned to Webster were starting to become like a close-knit little family, even Dick was becoming more like a human being and less like a walking asshat. She was closest with Sabine and Clarence, the three of them had formed a tight bond that she now cherished. Bianca was hard to read at times, she could be warm and fuzzy one minute and completely cold and closed off the next. Oscar was still his shy self, but each day he made a little more progress on opening up.

Added responsibilities were being passed to them everyday and Athena was thrilled about it. Each time she was paged to a patient's room to assess a situation or prescribe a medication, in her eyes validated that she actually belonged there. That she'd made it as a doctor and was on track to making her dreams a reality.

One Tuesday morning while she, Sabine and Clarence were in the teaching lab practicing their sutures, Sabine voiced the question that had been on all of their minds.

"So when do you think they'll let us cut?" she asked, raising an eyebrow. Her black hair was wrapped around her head in intricate braids that only she could pull off, giving her a soft yet sleek look. Athena knew for a fact there was more than one doctor in the hospital that had his—and maybe even a few hers—eye on her.

"I think it's gonna be today. I feel it, something big is gonna happen today," Clarence replied, nodding at them.

"I don't know. You think so? What could possibly happen that would get us all into the OR today with scalpels in our hands?" Athena asked, wondering if he knew something they didn't.

"You just gotta stay focused and positive and keep your eye on the prize. Me, I can just feel it—today's the day, you'll see." Clarence explained without really explaining. Sabine rolled her eyes behind his back and the three continued working in silence for several minutes.

"I bet that asswipe, Dick gets booted from the program before he even gets a chance to cut," Sabine said, looping her last stitch and cutting the string. "Bam. Cross stitch in the bag, bitches."

Athena giggled and went back to concentrating on practicing the new technique she was trying to master. If her big shot did come up, she wanted to be ready; no matter what. All three of their pagers went off at once before she could respond and glancing at hers, she saw she was being paged to the ER. A quick look at Sabine and Clarence told her that their pages were the same, which could only mean one thing. A trauma was coming in. Dropping their utensils, they hit the door at a run, eagerness and anticipation spurring them forward. Getting there first meant potentially getting assigned to a resident or attending that might end up in surgery, which would give them a chance at scrubbing in with them. Now that there were potential surgeries on the line, friendships were tossed aside as the three of them fought for the lead on their sprint to the emergency room.

Webster was waiting for them when they arrived and ordered them into the white trauma gowns that fit over their scrub uniforms. "There was a building collapse over on 32nd. We don't know how many injured yet but it's serious and we need all hands on deck. This is it," she turned to face them, her red hair swishing around her shoulders as she ushered them to the trauma entrance doors. "This is the biggest shot you'll have at proving you're not complete imbeciles and can be useful as doctors. Don't make me regret bringing you all down here," she raised her voice so that Bianca, Oscar and Dick who'd just joined them could hear.

Two ambulances pulled into the waiting bays at once, both sirens blaring. Paramedics leaped out, shouting out reports and rushing inside with the doctors that eagerly stepped forward to jump on the cases. Feeling intimidated, Athena hung back, unsure of herself. A few more arrivals and Sabine, Dick and Oscar had patients and were heading inside to better assess and treat the victims of the building collapse.

"You'll never learn anything dancing from foot to foot out here," a voice from behind told her. She knew from the light shivers that travelled down her spine who it was. His presence sent awareness tingling through her that she desperately tried to ignore. Her reaction to him was an unwanted distraction. The man was affecting her more than he should.

"I know. I just...well, the next one is mine. I was waiting—" Cian cut her off before she could say any more.

"Waiting doesn't do anyone any good, Payne," he leaned in closer, noting her sharp intake of breath and the way her olive eyes lit up. "If you see something you want, you've got to take it." Silence stretched between them as she stared up at him, chest heaving as her breath came in fast little beats. *Are we still talking about traumas?* she wondered to herself, the sneaking suspicion that their conversation had taken a turn into something more niggling at the back of her mind.

The next ambulance pulled in before she could pull together a reply, not that she was sure her brain was even functioning enough to form coherent words. Cian's dark eyes and sexy smirk were permanently burned in her memory. The man was too drool-worthy for his own good. She gave herself a small shake, ignoring the chuckle she heard behind her at her behavior, and snapped on a pair of gloves. The paramedic burst out of the ambulance, her right hand pumping hard on the oxygen mask fitted over a woman's mouth and shouting out information as they all rushed inside.

"Female victim, Samantha Chambers, thirty-two years old. Was crushed in the first wave of the collapse, rescue workers almost didn't find her. Several broken bones, severe damage to the chest area and we lost her in the bus on the way here. Got her back just as we pulled in. Pulse is holding strong now at sixty; but it was touch and go there for a minute." Cian nodded and then ordered her taken to trauma room two. Athena hung back, unsure if she should follow.

"You with me, Payne?" he called over his shoulder, not glancing her way. Excitement bubbled through her and she quickly jogged to catch up.

"Yes, sir. I'm with you. Are you worried about internal bleeding?" she asked.

"It's likely. I'm more worried about the stress her heart took under that concrete." Jenson, one of the newer residents was already in the room, calling out medications and barking orders at the nurses. Cian took over when he stepped in.

"Book a CT and let's see what's going on under there." He walked over to lean over Samantha's head. "Ms. Chambers, can you hear me?" her head was strapped down to the backboard to keep her still, but her eyes were wide with shock and fright.

"Yes. Yes, the building! Oh, God. The screaming. Did everyone make it out? Am I going to be okay? I can't feel my body at all, is my body still there?" she tried to glance down but was unable to due to the restraints. "I'm missing aren't I? Oh, God, oh, God." The alarms on the monitors blared as Samantha's eyes rolled back in her head and her body began to quake.

"She's seizing!" Athena yelled out and everyone rushed around at once, pumping medications and talking to each other at once.

"Call and book an OR now," Cian ordered Athena.

"Yes, Dr. O'Reilly," she replied, moving to do just that.

"And then get back here, you're scrubbing in."

Thrilled, she dashed through the ER to the nurses' desk and snatched up the phone, securing the OR as ordered. Looking around, the department was alive with screams and wails of the injured, crying from visitors as they were reunited with missing loved ones and doctors giving orders to nurses and interns alike. There was nothing like the feeling of pride that went through her for being a part of something so magnificent. The power to save lives, to heal, to help people when they needed it most. That's what she had now. What she was a part of. A warrior in a pair of scrubs and gloves, she was determined to keep pushing herself until she became the best of the best. A doctor that families trusted and colleagues respected. For now, there was a young woman in there that was fighting for her life and it was her job to go and make sure they saved it.

Some ten minutes later, they were scrubbed and in the OR, ready to begin. She hung back at Cian's elbow, off to the right so that she could still observe everything that he did. When the cut area was prepped, he shifted his feet and called out for a scalpel. Placing the blade to her skin, he suddenly stopped and stepped back.

"Payne."

Payne? That was her name.

"Um, sir?"

"Get over here. You're making the first incision." Gasps echoed around the room as his words sunk in. Never before had Dr. O'Reilly handed over the knife. For him to allow someone else to make the first incision was unheard of, especially an intern. Dumbfounded, Athena stayed rooted to the spot, unsure if she'd actually heard him correctly.

"Move it, Payne. We don't have time to waste here."

She shuffled forward and stood to Cian's left, looking at him with questions in her eyes. He handed her the scalpel and with his hand on top of hers, guided her to the correct starting place on Samantha's chest.

"You're going to press down here. Skin is tough, so you need to apply a little bit of pressure, but not a lot. Just enough to break through. Keep your hand steady and move in a horizontal line to here," he indicated where she needed to stop with his other hand. "You've been practicing in the labs, correct?"

"Yes, Dr. O'Reilly. Everyday."

"Good. That's good. Well, Payne, it's time to take the training wheels off, you ready?" She nodded profusely, more ready than anything ever in her life. With his hand lightly on top of hers, she pressed down with the scalpel exactly how he'd instructed and then slowly moved it down. Blood immediately sprang to the surface and coated both their fingers as she completed the first cut of her career.

Looking up at him for approval, something passed between them in the clash of her olive eyes to his dark. Standing in a room where life met death, both their hands coated in blood; it was a powerful moment. He'd just given her something she'd always remember, her first cut as a surgeon. No words were exchanged between them, yet their connection grew in just those few seconds.

"Good work," he muttered and indicated for her to step back as he took over. Athena complied and after putting the scalpel in the sterile container, moved to the side to give herself a few moments to find her composure. She was in trouble where he was concerned. Deep fucking trouble.

"I can't fucking believe it!" Sabine slammed her sandwich down on the table before taking her seat beside Athena. "Not only did you get in the OR before me, you got your first cut before me too! Who do I have to fuck around here to get some goddamn recognition?"

"That's not how it works, Sabine, you know that. We just have to wait for that right opportunity to come along, I guess. Who knew that Clarence would actually be right and today something big would happen to get a few of us in the OR. I just never thought it would be Cian that would give me my first—"

"Wait just a fucking minute! Cian?! He's the reason you got your first cut today? Jesus fuck, your pussy power knows no bounds, girl! He actually gave you the scalpel? Fuck me, I need to spend more time with that man."

"Ugh, that's not how it happened. I don't even know how it happened. He was just there, encouraging me and the next thing I knew, I was cutting for the first time. As much as I'm grateful he gave me the chance, there's something about him, Sab. Something off. There's a darkness in him and I'm not sure what to think about that."

Frustrated that her best friend was making light of a situation that truly had her conflicted, Athena stood up and tossed her remaining soup in the trash; her appetite gone. She knew Sabine was only teasing about her 'pussy power', but it didn't make it any easier of a pill to swallow. The rumors would begin to fly again like they had been since her first encounter with Cian, she had no doubt about that.

"I know that isn't how it happened, Thene. I'm just giving you shit. I'm jealous as fuck and dying for you to move things along with Mr. Dark and Dangerous."

"There's nothing to move along. He's my boss. He's your boss. He's our boss's boss. I want him to teach me to be the best cardiothoracic surgeon I can be...that's all I want from him."

"Well anyone with eyeballs can see that's not all he wants from you. Mark my words, Athena, he's coming for you."

chapter eight

THE MOST DIFFICULT part of the hunt was choosing his victims. As despicable as it was, there were hundreds of criminals who escaped punishments for their crimes every day. His wife's murderers were among that group and it was an injustice that burned in Cian's blood with every breath he took. When he re-awakened in the hospital after finding her body, he'd been enraged to find out that the two fuckers that stole his beautiful wife from him had gotten away. Despite the investigation and the large reward he'd offered, the police never apprehended them. They got away with their crime just as so many others did. It was his mission to one day find them and get them both on his table; he'd relish in the kill and sending them to the hell they deserved. Flipping open his notebook, he reviewed the information on their next victim.

Lana Fraser, age 27
906 Carver, Queens
Former nurse at Lincoln Hospital
Accused of overdosing and poisoning patients. Arrested on charges of assault to a body on
deceased patients. Suspected in the suspicious deaths of over fifty patients. Released on
insufficient amount of evidence after her arrest

He remembered Lana, a snotty, dark-haired cunt that rubbed almost everyone in the hospital the wrong way. She looked down her nose at patients, residents, even attendings'. Her smartass attitude was not appreciated and definitely earned her more than one enemy. She upset families almost every shift, the complaints about her a mile long. He recalled one family in particular that just wanted their mother to have a sip of water after having a test and drinking that horrible tasting dye. She refused to call the doctor and have the patient taken off the nothing by mouth order, ignoring the family when they explained they had been told water would be fine for her to have after the test. The family was in a state of shock after just learning their mother had stage four cancer, when they were only in hospital for routine tests. The complete lack of compassion Lana showed was enough to have the youngest daughter, a little firecracker, take the issue all the way to the nurse manager on the floor. It was her complaints about Lana's behavior and treatment of other patients that finally had the hospital looking at her more closely and discovering what she'd done.

She'd been immediately fired and the police had been informed, but without hard evidence, it was nearly impossible to get the D.A.'s office to file charges. In the end, Lana was set free, but the hospital maintained its position on firing her. A fact that she was now suing them over on the grounds of wrongful dismissal.

Tonight, she would finally answer for her crimes, he would show her no mercy and she'd know what it was like to be on the receiving end of no compassion. Everything was set and ready to go. He'd created an online dating profile after stalking her Facebook page and discovering that she used one of those sites to look for men. It was sickeningly easy the way he'd been able to make a fake profile and used it to connect with her. If he ever had a daughter, he'd make damn sure—

The deep stabbing pain at his innocent thought sliced through him. Having a daughter wasn't something he had to worry about now, not since...not since Hannah had been murdered. Her face swam before his eyes and the agony at recalling her smile and the way she used to laugh just about broke him.

Furious with himself for letting her memory slip through the walls he had up, he slammed his notebook closed and headed to his bathroom to shower and get ready to pick up the package and get to the hospital. It was a change of rotation in shifts, so they'd be starting their day with Lana's disposal, instead of ending it like usual. This would be the first time of them trying this on the new schedule and everything had to be perfect to avoid any problems. He was keyed up, antsy and ready to get started, the need to kill was slowly eating him alive from the inside out.

Keeping up his facade was starting to wear on him. Cian was not a man used to denying himself any of his wants and needs. And what he wanted, what he craved, was to strip away the layers of his humanity; the disguise of profession. The monster within was clawing at him from the inside, desperate to be unleashed.

Hunt.

Maim.

Kill.

The bitch was going to suffer before she met her end.

A few hours later, Cian sat parked in his car across from the pub where he'd arranged to meet Lana. He could see her seated at a table by herself through one of the big windows. Every now and then she checked her watch, a telltale sign to everyone in the bar that she'd been stood up. Chuckling, he took a moment to enjoy the extra little bit of torture he was inflicting on her. No woman wanted to be stood up and he felt a twinge of pity for the poor waitress that had to suffer her wrath every time she stopped by the table to check on Lana.

When she finally gave up and stepped out of the bar, it was time for Cian to make his move. He climbed out of the car and quickened his pace to catch up with her. When he was a foot behind, he slipped the needle from his pocket and reaching her side, smoothly slid it into her bare arm. After a few steps, she began to slump down and Cian immediately put his arm around her to prop her up into his side. A few curious onlookers stopped to glance their way, but he flashed a dazzling smile and put them at ease.

"My girlfriend's had a bit too much tonight, time for me to put her to bed, I think. These damned girl's nights out," he laughed, giving off the attitude of a caring boyfriend. A few of the men shared knowing glances.

"You need a hand with her, man?"

"Nah. I got it. Thanks though, I appreciate it. Come on, sweets. Let's get you home." He steered Lana in the direction of his car and once she was seated safely in his passenger seat, a devious grin spread across his face. That had been way too fucking easy. Lana moaned and her head lolled on her shoulder, giving the impression to anyone that passed them that she was asleep. Pleased with himself, Cian pulled away from the curb and headed in the direction of the hospital. At the rendezvous point, he steered off the road and into an abandoned parking lot. Reynolds was waiting there with his car and if he'd followed instructions, it would be lined with plastic and ready to go.

He cut the engine and rounded the hood to the passenger side to pull Lana out and dump her unceremoniously onto the asphalt. Reynolds handed him the knife without a word and Cian lifted Lana's head up, trying to bring her around. When he was unsuccessful, he shrugged and in one powerful thrust, stabbed her in the gut. Lana grunted but otherwise made no other movements.

"That outta get things rolling," Cian commented and together he and Reynolds lifted her and put her in Reynolds' car.

"Now, just as we discussed. Dump her a few feet from the entrance and I'll come out and find her while you circle back and come in the hospital from the other side. Patricia and Lorna should have everything set in the OR, I'll text now and be sure."

"I got it. See you there in ten."

Cian pulled out his phone and sent a quick message to Patricia. Ever since the meeting they'd had at his apartment a few weeks ago regarding the vigilante reports on the news, he was more sure than ever that it wasn't a member of his team that was leaking information. Either Rae Kelley was just really fucking intuitive, which was highly unlikely, or someone knew their secret. Now the question was, why weren't they saying anything?

Patricia messaged back that everyone was in place and satisfied, he got back in the car and headed to meet his first patient of the evening.

Walking into the ER, he stopped by the nurse's desk to flirt with the pretty receptionist he'd never seen before. He was close to charming her number out of her when the squeal of tires outside caught his attention and he ran out the doors to investigate. Finding Lana laying crumpled on the pavement, he called out for help while silently cheering on the inside. The plan had worked perfectly. In seconds, she was on the gurney and being transferred to his playground.

"Page Reynolds and get him to meet me in OR-B!" he yelled as they hurried down the hall, she really was losing a lot of blood fast and they had to hurry if he was going to be able to accomplish what he had planned for her.

Athena stepped into the hall a few feet behind him, watching the scene with interest. She found it curious that he didn't call for a resident or an intern as was his norm when he had an emergent case. She'd been observing him for weeks now and knew that was his usual habit. So for something this serious to come in and him to handle it on his own, pricked at her curiosity. Intent on following him and observing the procedure from the scrub room, she started down the hall after them only to skid to a halt when her name was yelled out.

"Payne! Get over here," Webster shouted from across the department.

Cian heard her as well and turning his head, locked eyes with Athena. For a split second she thought she saw something like guilt flash in his eyes but then it was gone and he shut down. His brown eyes turned black again and he gave her his back without so much as a word.

"The patients in rooms 7B, 22A and 16A need to be checked in on and 32B needs a drain changed. Mysteriously, all of our other interns have disappeared so you have them to thank that all those jobs are yours. I hope you have a good memory as I don't—"

"Repeat yourself. I got it, Dr. Webster. I'll take care of it." Disappointed that she wouldn't be able to lurk around Cian's surgery and see what the deal was, she headed off to follow Webster's orders. She was going to kill Sabine and the others for ducking off who knew where and leaving her with all the work. What a way to start a shift.

Cian finished scrubbing and entered the OR. Everyone was in place and except for the almost hiccup with Athena following them, it had all gone according to plan.

Lana was awake if her trashing on the table was any indication. Her grunts of pain from behind the gag increased with every push of her body off the table as she struggled to get free. All she was doing of course was worsening her own pain as she caused the slash in her abdomen to enlarge.

"Ah, Lana, good to see you again. You remember me, I hope?" Cian asked as he peered at her from his place at the side of the OR table. Lana shook her head wildly, her moans getting louder. The glazed look in her eyes and the pool of blood on the floor told him they had even less time than he thought before she bled out.

"Peroxide," he ordered and took the bottle from Lorna when she passed it to him. "So, Lana. I hear that poison was your choice way to murder patients in this hospital. What a way for those poor suckers to go. Tell me, why? Why did you do such a thing? Were you just born without a heart?" Not waiting for a reply, he poured a generous amount of the peroxide into her open wound watching as her blood sizzled and her skin seemed to burn.

"I particularly remember a story of you being cruel to a family that had just received devastating news. I bet they'd love to see you suffer like this now, they way you made them suffer back then. Pliers."

He accepted the pliers from Patricia and spreading open the large gash in her stomach, grasped a piece of her large intestine and pulled, stretching it until it was almost out of her body. Lana jerked once and then went completely still, the monitor indicating that she had flat-lined.

"Goddammit!" Cian swore, furious. "Get her back," he ordered Reynolds.

"Cian, be reasonable. It's done and we're short on time as it is."

"Fuck. Fuck, fuck!" It had barely been long enough for him to feel his need satisfied. The devious part of him raged at being cut short and before he did something he would later regret, he stomped out of the OR, ordering them to take care of things.

Athena had just stepped out of a patient room when Cian came charging down the hall. Spotting her, he barreled forward, latching onto her arm and not stopping, dragging her behind him in his wake. Pure rage was in every step he took and Athena could barely keep up with his long-legged stride. When he reached the on-call room, he threw the door open, shoved her inside and then slammed and locked the door behind them.

"Cian? Um, I mean, Dr. O'Reilly. What's going on?" Completely bewildered and a tad terrified at his behavior, she backed away from him a few steps. He stalked forward for every step she took back and they ended up in a dance around the small room until her back hit the wall, leaving her no more options to avoid him.

"Um..." she bit her lower lip nervously and wondered what the fuck was going on. Had she done something wrong? Made a mistake? Maybe—

All thoughts flew out of her mind when with a brutal growl, his mouth swooped down on hers to claim her lips in a soul-consuming kiss. It was a kiss not about passion; but about possession. His hands dug into her waist painfully as he dragged her against his chest, fusing their bodies together. His tongue wasn't going to be denied as he pushed past her lips and tasted every inch of her mouth. Her head spun and her pulse raced. Such a devouring kiss stole every part of her she'd tried to keep for herself. He was taking over; owning her and branding her as his. In that moment, she had no idea where he ended and she began. As much as she was scared, her body felt alive and she began to respond to his touch.

Her hands found their way around his neck and into his hair as she raised on her tiptoes to get closer. She met him head on, riding on the power of their connection and the taste of him on her tongue. She'd never known that vulnerability could be such a high endorphin. And that's what he was whether he chose to admit it or not; he was vulnerable and looking for something to latch on to.

His hand traveled under her scrub top and found her breasts, pinching and tugging her nipples through her bra as he ground his hips against hers. Without realizing it, she hoisted herself up and wrapped her legs around his trim waist, desperate to feel more friction between her legs. The second she felt his hard cock against her pussy with only their thin clothes separating them; she moaned into his mouth and rocked against him slowly. Cian brought one hand up and tugging her hair, exposed her neck to him. He dragged his mouth from hers and sank his teeth into her tender flesh, intent on marking her as his.

"Cian," she breathed out his name and he stilled, his body freezing. He let her drop down to the ground and then stepped back, his own breath coming in shallow pants.

She looked at him with questions in her eyes, not sure why he'd stopped when they both so clearly wanted to continue.

"Get out." he barked and she flinched at his tone. Shame filled her along with embarrassment as she hastily straightened her clothes. Maybe she was a terrible kisser or had done something he didn't like. Whatever the reason, he obviously wanted her out of his sight.

She rushed to the door, misery in every step. She needed to get as far from him as she could.

"And don't ever fucking think of following me again." His parting words cut like a knife and cleared all fog of desire from her brain.

Cian O'Reilly wasn't a good man at all. He was a monster, plain and simple.

chapter nine

"I'M JUST SAYING, Thene, you two have danced around each other for almost three weeks now. When are you going to get over it and call him out on his asshole move?" Sabine asked in a low voice one morning as they followed behind Webster and the other interns. They were doing their routine rounds and next for them to see was Sebastian, the little boy who'd stolen her heart the first time she'd met him.

"I'm not, Sab. It was a momentary lapse in judgement on my part and I won't let it happen again. All dealings between C— Dr. O'Reilly and I will be strictly professional. I need him to be my teacher; nothing more." Sabine had switched from team get-Cian-in-Athena's-pants to team I-want-to-kill-him-for-hurting-Athena in a matter of seconds after finding out about what had happened in the on-call room. It'd taken everything Athena had to talk her down and get her to cease and desist before she hunted Cian down and cut off his balls like she wanted to. That was what Athena loved about Sabine, her fire and her loyalty. She couldn't have asked for a better best friend.

"Good morning, Sebastian, Mrs. Harris," Webster greeted them as they stepped into the five-year-old's room. They had been rounding on the Harris family every morning and Athena had formed a tight bond with Sebastian. He was the sweetest little boy, a real sports nut and had a love of the outdoors. Mrs. Harris was a widow; her husband had been killed the year before in a car wreck. She spent every waking hour at the hospital, only taking a break when she needed to tend to some matters at their home. Athena couldn't imagine what the stress of worrying about her child dying was doing to her, especially on the heels of the fresh grief of losing her husband.

She often snuck in on her down time to bring Sebastian new coloring books or play a quick game of Crazy Eight's, his favorite card game. He somehow had it in his head that it was actually poker and she didn't have the heart to set him straight.

"Good morning, Dr. Webster. Hi, team," Mara Harris greeted them the same way she did every morning. The toll of waiting on a new heart for Sebastian was starting to show in the dullness of her hair and the worry lines around her eyes.

"Athena!" Sebastian exclaimed when he saw her. His voice lacked its usual enthusiasm and his coloring was more gray than usual. He was growing more and more sick by the day and if they didn't get him a heart soon; Athena feared their worst nightmare was going to come true.

"Hey, little man," she greeted him. He grinned but it didn't quite reach his eyes this time, a fact that broke her heart. He was only five, he should be out playing t-ball and chasing frogs—not lying in a hospital bed waiting on a miracle just so he could live.

"Can we play poker later when you're hiding from work?" he asked, earning her a raised eyebrow from Webster. She laughed nervously and twirled a lock of her hair. Dick snickered and she wanted to kick him.

"When I'm on my *break,* yes we can definitely play poker." she corrected him.

"Maybe instead of teaching children to play poker you should be worrying about their medical care," a voice called out from the doorway. She knew it was him, she'd know that voice anywhere, despite her best efforts to forget he existed.

"Poker is code for Crazy Eights," she answered without meeting his eyes. If he wanted to think she wasn't prepped on Sebastian's case; let him. She'd answer any damn question he threw at her. She took a deep breath to calm her nerves and paid attention to the update on Sebastian's care. When they were finished, she told Sebastian she'd see him later and since he was the last patient they had to round on, used the free moment to escape into the unusually empty lab.

Damn him. He had a way of affecting her like no other. He'd made it clear he didn't want anything to do with her so why did she care what he thought?

Pacing the room, lost in her thoughts, she didn't notice the figure behind her until a shadow fell over her and arms encircled her; clamping down and trapping her arms to her sides.

Hot breath whispered in her ear and sent a chill of fear down her spine. "Well, well, what do we have here? A hot as fuck piece of ass doctor all by herself," the voice was unfamiliar and full of malice.

"H—" she started to scream but was cut off when his hand slapped over her mouth and pulled her head back against him roughly. His other hand worked its way down the front of her body and into her scrub pants, rubbing her pussy roughly over her panties.

"You don't want to go screaming and ruining our fun now do you, lady doc?" His tongue licked her ear and she recoiled away from him, struggling as much as she could to get out of his hold.

Terror gripped her, but she knew she had to fight if she wanted to get away unharmed. She stomped down hard on his foot and then drove her elbow into his stomach, elated when he loosened his hold enough for her to get free and make a break for the door. Just as she reached for the handle, he latched onto her again, this time grabbing her hair and dragging her back. She stumbled and landed in a heap on her ass, crab-walking backwards to try and escape. He grabbed her by the arm and pulled her to her feet. Shoving her down on the lab table, he grunted as his actions sent glass crashing to the floor around them.

"Please. What do you want?" she asked, hoping to keep him talking. His blue eyes were manic and his long dirty hair hung over his face as he stared down at her.

"You fucking people cut off my medication and I need it. I can't survive without it; don't you see?" He pulled a large cutting knife from the waistband of his jeans and waved it in front of her face. "I don't want to hurt you, but I will if you don't give me what I need." He pressed harder between her legs and Athena felt tears drip from her eyes his erection rubbed against her.

"Please. Please don't do this," she begged as he pushed the knife to her neck and started fumbling with her pants managing to drag them and her panties down to her knees.

"You want it. They all fucking want it, fucking whores," he mumbled. He got his jeans down to his ankles and no matter how hard she bucked, she felt the tip of him at her entrance and she began to scream, not caring if he cut her.

Suddenly, his weight was lifted off her and a gush of cold air hit her. She had a second to sit up and see Cian there struggling with her attacker. The man swiped out with the knife once and Cian jumped back to avoid the slash. To her amazement and horror, he rushed forward, taking the man by surprise and in one swift movement, snapped his neck. The attacker fell to the ground, his neck bent at an odd angle and his cold, dead eyes locked on her.

"Oh, God, oh, God! You...you killed him! He came in here and I was in here and then I ran but I fell and then the knife and my pants but you...you killed him," she babbled, shock starting to set in.

Cian approached her slowly and pulled her pants up her legs, covering her. "Athena. It's okay. You're safe, I promise, it's okay now." Hearing those words broke the dam and loud, choking sobs ripped from her throat as she threw herself forward into his arms and cried into his chest.

"Thank you. Thank you," she mumbled against him. Her tears soaking his shirt did something to Cian. The coldness around his heart began to crack and thaw a little as this brave woman broke and clung to him for support. She was a fighter and would have kept fighting even if he hadn't heard the commotion and investigated. The pure violent fury he'd felt when he saw that fucking cocksucker on top of her had been enough to propel him forward and end his life. He wished now that he'd had more time with him, but the deed was done and Athena was safe. That was what mattered.

He helped her stand and together the left the lab, Cian ordering the receptionist at the main desk to call the police. He led Athena to the attendings' lounge and got her a cup of water before paging Sabine. She'd want her best friend there to lean on while she gave her statement to the police.

Twenty minutes later, two detectives entered the lounge, one male, one female. The female was an older woman with hair just starting to gray pulled back in a low bun. The male was much younger, probably early thirties and handsome with dark hair and blue eyes. He approached Athena first and sat down in a chair across from her.

"Dr. Payne? I'm Detective Seth Holloway and this is my partner, Detective Janet Babb. We need to ask you a few questions about what happened, are you feeling up to that?" His tone was kind and his eyes full of compassion as he watched her. Something about him immediately put her at ease and she nodded, not trusting herself to speak at that moment for fear she might burst into tears again. She needed just a few more minutes to compose herself.

The door banged open and Sabine flew in like a hurricane. "Where is he? Where is the fuck that hurt you? I'll kill him, I swear to God I'll tear his limbs off like chicken bones and feed them to the dogs," Sabine spit out, her eyes darting all around the room as if she expected her attacker to materialize at any second.

"Sabine," she croaked, her throat raw from holding back the tears. "I'm fine. He's..." her eyes met Cian's, "he's gone."

"You're damn right he better be gone. In handcuffs carted off to prison where he belongs," she glared at the two cops and crossed her arms over her chest. "Well? Why aren't you carting him off?" she demanded.

"Because I fucking killed the son-of-a-bitch," Cian told her, exasperated with the entire situation.

Sabine sank down on the sofa beside Athena. "Well okay then," she replied, calm for the moment.

Detective Holloway cleared his throat. "Can we get started now, Athena? Tell me what happened when you entered the lab."

She recounted everything she remembered, wrapping her arms around her stomach and rocking slightly when she explained in precise detail how he'd assaulted her. Cian's blood boiled hearing what he'd done and tried to do and he severely wished he could kill the fucker all over again. Thank fuck he'd got there when he did.

"And that's when you came in, Dr. O'Reilly?" Holloway asked. The man was regarding him with intelligent eyes and a friendly smile. Cian was no fool though and while it may have been justified, he'd still killed a man and needed to be sure he was as accurate as possible in his re-telling of the events.

"Yes. I found the assailant on top of Dr. Payne..."

Athena tuned out Cian's explanation of what he'd done, not needing to hear the words. The image would be forever burned in her memory; she saw the man's face every time she closed her eyes.

Sabine's pager went off and she swore. "I gotta go, but I'll be back." She kissed Athena's forehead and then surprised everybody by standing and wrapping Cian in a bear hug. "Thank you. We're each other's only family, so...just thank you." she said simply and then walked out.

Detective Holloway stood and placed a comforting hand on Athena's shoulder. "I think we have everything we need for now. I want you to go home and try to relax. Here's my card." He handed her a small white business card. "Call me if you need anything at all, night or day." He snatched it back out of her hand and scribbled something on it. "That's my personal cell as well. Just in case." Athena stared up at him, unsure but wondering if he was hitting on her. When he just smiled that kind smile again, she brushed it aside and thanked him for everything. "Stay available in case we need you for anything, Dr. O'Reilly," Babb told him and then they left the room.

"Do you need a ride home?" Cian asked her as soon as they were alone. She looked so fragile and scared sitting there. The urge to gather her back into his arms was strong, but he kept his distance.

"I'm fine. My friend will take me," she replied, not looking up. He turned to leave and then took one last look at her, fighting against every instinct to stay and comfort her. Just as he stepped in the hall, she called him back.

"Cian. Thank you, you saved my life." He nodded and then left her sitting there alone.

Athena's hand visibly shook as she poured herself a healthy glass of wine later that night in the safety of her high-rise apartment.

She'd lied to Cian when she told him she had a ride home. Conflicted by what she felt after he saved her, she hadn't wanted to be alone with him. Instead, she drove herself home which in hindsight wasn't a smart idea. Her hands had shaken the entire time and she'd nearly caused several accidents. Now that she was safely home, what she needed most was a lot of wine and a soak in her tub to wash away the horror of what had nearly happened to her.

She flashed back to the disgusting man's hands on her, the filthy things he'd whispered in her ear, the feel of the cold steel of the knife pressed against her throat. Shuddering, she gulped the wine and took a few deep breaths. If Cian—Dr. O'Reilly—hadn't got to her when he did, who knows what would have happened. The thought had tremors running through her as she fought to shake off the chill.

Heading to the bathroom to make good on her plan to wash the memories away in a soothing bubble bath; Cian's cold eyes crept into her mind. The undiluted rage she'd seen, the concise way he'd disposed of her attacker with precision...well it was a little unnerving, no matter how grateful she was. There was a darkness simmering in him, something beneath the surface that he fought hard to conceal. As terrifying as it was, it was also alluring in a way. Seductive even. Something about his savage skills was damn sexy.

"Get ahold of yourself, you imbecile," she muttered. Lusting after a man that had killed another human that very day, and was her boss no less. It was ridiculous. She was ridiculous. He'd made it clear after their one steamy make-out session that he didn't want anything to do with her on a romantic level.

A knock on her apartment door startled her and had wine sloshing over the rim of her glass. Panic gripped her as she irrationally thought it was her attacker, before remembering that he was dead.

"Athena." Cian's strong voice flowed from behind the door. "Let me in." Oh, God it was Cian. What the hell was he doing there? Frantic, she looked in the mirror. Her dark tresses were piled on top of her head in a lopsided bun that she quickly tightened into place. Her face had been washed clean of all make-up and she was wearing a ratty, oversized t-shirt that fell to her knees. It was one of her favorite and made the perfect comfy nightgown. With no time to dash to her room to change, she sighed and pulled open the door.

"What are you doing here?" she asked straight away. He was holding two white bags that smelled suspiciously like burgers and fries.

He pushed his way inside and kicked the door closed behind him before answering. "Well when Sabine and I found out that you drove yourself home," that earned her a stern glare. "We flipped a coin on who would get to come over here to yell at you. I won," he explained. "I decided to show you a little mercy and figured since you'd likely be drowning yourself in some sort of alcohol, I'd pick up some dinner. Sabine said this was your weakness," he lifted the bags.

Athena was shocked. He was actually being kind to her, talking to her like she was an actual human being instead of just an intern.

"Um, yah it is. Well, come in," she invited, leading him to the living room where he sat on her black leather sofa and she went to the kitchen to pour him a glass of wine and grab a couple of plates.

Joining him in the living room, she handed him the wine and then dug into the take-out bags, sharing out the burgers and fries between them. They ate in silence for a few moments, Athena praying that he wouldn't notice the way her hands were still shaking. Of course, that didn't happen as this was Cian and he never missed a thing.

He placed his hand over hers and rested the other on her cheek, turning her to face him. "Hey. You okay?"

She nodded jerkily and pulled her gaze from his, not wanting to get lost in the dark pools of his stare.

"I thought he was going to kill me," she whispered, putting her burger down. The food was starting to come back up her throat and she didn't want to embarrass herself by barfing all over the man.

"I know. I was worried there for a moment as well. But, Athena, he's gone now and you're safe. I promise." He took her hand and her fingers automatically intertwined with his, the chemistry sizzled between them and it was a Herculean effort on his part to not scoop her into his arms and kiss her senseless once again.

She looked up at him and the naked vulnerability in her eyes was almost his undoing. Before he did something neither of them could take back, he stood up and headed for the door. She followed him, confused at his abrupt change.

At the door, he turned to her and kissed her forehead before opening it and stepping into the hallway. "Get some rest. Lock up," he said and then he was gone.

Athena did as he said and then leaned against the wall, letting her head fall back. "Oh no, that doesn't complicate things at all. Fuck."

chapter ten

LAYLA HUNT WAS close to giving up. She had no idea how long it'd been now since she'd been taken prisoner by the two sick fucks that had her, but it definitely felt like a lifetime. The longer she was held in captivity by the two madmen, the more she lost hope that she'd ever escape or be set free. Her body held the scars of their fetish; their obsession with blood. The younger man, Dane, had inflicted dozens of cuts, stabbed her superficially multiple times. Never deep enough to cause serious damage, but painful enough so that she felt it and he got his taste of her blood.

The older man, Marcus, was the more sadistic of the two. He preferred to watch and instruct which in her mind made him all the more dangerous. He was very careful to rarely touch her or partake in the torture that Dane put her through. Dane had abused her, but had yet to rape her. Each day it went farther and farther and she knew it wouldn't be long before it happened. The thought terrified her as she knew she wouldn't survive being forced against her will. She had to keep her strength up and find a way out of the house she was being held in before the unthinkable happened.

Since she'd been moved a few weeks ago—at least she thought it'd been a few weeks—she was now kept in a small bedroom, her ankle attached to a short chain that allowed her just enough freedom to walk to the adjoining bathroom and back. At least she'd been given the luxury of a toilet, when she's first been taken she'd only been given a stainless steel bucket. It was humiliating.

She knew that she wasn't the only captive in the house, she'd heard the screams, the begging for help, the pleas for mercy. Several of the women seemed to have it worse off than she did if their cries were any indication. She hoped like hell that the opportunity to escape presented itself; she wouldn't rest until every one of those women were free.

She got that determination from her father. A firefighter, he'd worked his way up the ranks until he became Chief, an accomplishment he was so proud of. His marriage to her mother was a rocky one. Ghosts from the past constantly rose up and got between them, causing more than once for one of them to walk away, stating that it was over between them before it even started. Their love always held though and they conquered their differences and patched things up. Layla feared that if anything happened to her, all bets in that department would be off.

The door to her room opened and Dane entered, a huge grin on his face. "And how is my little Lay Lay today? Ha, I rhymed." Dane laughed at his own joke and closed the door behind him, clicking the lock into place.

"Fuck off," she spat back, not in the mood for him at all.

"Yep, same smart mouth as always. God, I love that about you. Wonder if that's a trait you get from your mother or your father?" He waved his hand at her, indicating he didn't expect a response to his question.

"You brought another girl here," she accused, furious that he was still getting away with what he was doing.

"You really never miss a thing do you, darlin'?" he chuckled and then withdrew the machete from behind his back. Layla's eyes bugged out of her head at the sight of it. She'd never seen him come in with a weapon like that before.

"Ah, this got a reaction from you, didn't it?" His grin was cold, wicked delight at the fear springing to life in her eyes.

"W—what are you going to do with that?" she stammered out, afraid to hear the answer.

"Well, I thought I'd start by..." he didn't finish his sentence, just charged forward and lashed out, slicing down her arm in one fluid movement.

"Ahhhhhhhh!" she screamed, jumping back and trying to clutch the entire gash with one hand. "Stop, stop, fuck!" she cried out as he repeated the motion on her other arm. Both were now gushing with blood and he stood there greedily taking in the sight.

As he started to reach for her, no doubt to spread his hands through her blood like he always did, two things happened at once. Layla moved forward instead of backwards and surprised, Dane went to sidestep and tripped knocking into her and toppling them both to the ground. Seizing the surprise opportunity, Layla quickly grabbed the chain restraining her ankle and wound it around Dane's neck; pulling it tight.

Dane's face turned purple as his oxygen was cut off. Layla patted him down with her other hand and nearly squealed with delight when she found the keys to the cuff. Dane's head fell back and she knew he'd passed out, giving her just the freedom she needed to unlock herself.

Once free, she stood, swaying and nearly passing out herself. Every instinct screamed at her to hurry, that if she wanted to get away, she needed to fucking move her ass. Unlocking the door, she chanced one last look at Dane before running from the room, down the stairs and to the main door of the house. Leaving all the other girls behind felt wrong, but there was nothing she could do for them when she was bleeding so profusely and didn't have any help. She sent them a silent vow that she'd be back for them and then wrenched open the main door and ran like hell.

Freedom had never tasted so sweet and fresh air had never felt so good hitting her face. At the first house she came across, she ran up the front steps and pounded on the door.

"Help! Please, please let me in!" Thanking fuck when the door opened and a middle-aged man's jaw dropped when he took in the sight over her covered head to toe in blood, she fell into his arms.

"Please call the police. My name is Layla Hunt and I was kidnapped. I—they—we need your help," she begged before passing out cold.

"Jesus Christ!" he exclaimed. "Honey!" he yelled to his wife. "Call the police now! It's one of those missing girls!"

chapter eleven

TWO MONTHS PASSED without further incident at the hospital. Cian's team fell into a routine on the new schedule and his "packages" had two more successful surgeries resulting in the extermination of more criminals. His need to hunt was being satisfied, his desire to kill being fulfilled. The news reports on *The Watcher* seemed to die down after that young woman, Layla Hunt had escaped and been rescued. It had been front page news on all the papers how she'd managed to get free and and identify the killers. By the time police descended on the house she led them to, however, it was too late and they'd fled, leaving behind a house of bodies. The news had devastated those families that still held out hope that the missing women would come home safe and sound.

It was a complete bloodbath, the violence in the marks on the girls showed that they'd been killed in a rage, likely to help them distract authorities enough for them to make their getaway. As the sole survivor, Layla Hunt was going to have a long road of survivor's guilt ahead of her. The reports stated that she was back home with her family and receiving care for all that she'd endured.

Athena seemed to have bounced back after the attack on her in the lab. She'd thrown herself into her studying and increased her time practicing her skills and assisting on any and every case; no matter the specialty. On their run-ins, neither mentioned that he'd shown up at her place that night, each preferring to live in their bubble that there was nothing more than a professional relationship between them. He'd noticed Detective Holloway at the hospital a few times to see her, but when he'd made inquiries, the answer had been that it was related to the case.

Seeing them together annoyed the hell out of him. Why was it that she could talk to him about the attack and how she was feeling but when he casually asked, she gave him a smile that didn't reach those olive eyes and the standard, "I'm fine." He'd never detested the word 'fine' more than he did when it fell from her lips.

At the end of shift, he changed clothes in the attendings' lounge and when he came out, fell into step behind Athena and Sabine. Both were dressed in regular clothes, curls bouncing in Athena's dark brown hair and Sabine's black hair as they walked down the long hallway towards the exit. He couldn't keep his eyes off the way her jeans hugged her tight little ass, the gentle sway of her hips distracting him to the point where it took all of his self-control not to drag her off into the nearest empty room and get his hands on her.

Distracted, he only caught pieces of their conversation. "— we need this. A few drinks and a chance to unwind. We haven't had a day off in weeks and I for one plan to take full advantage of the one we have tomorrow by indulging in the three B's. Booze, boys and boy-I-can't-wait-to-get-you-home-and-into-my-bed." Sabine said on a giggle.

Athena hit her arm and Cian imagined she was rolling her eyes as she tended to do quite often around her best friend. The thought of the two of them dolled up and out on the prowl for one-night stands infuriated him. Some slobbering, numbskull was going to get the chance to have Athena in his arms? To sink his cock into her and capture her moans as she came? Oh, hell no. If she needed sexual release, she could get it from him. Not some bumbling idiot that wouldn't know his dick from the end of a broomstick. Quickening his step, he was about to drag her aside, when he got a hold of himself. What the hell was his problem? When did he turn into a possessive jackass over a woman who wasn't even his. Thoroughly disgusted with himself, he pulled back and let them go. They disappeared out the door in a flurry of chatter and giggles and he stood stupidly in the hall staring after them for a few minutes.

"Fuck it," he said out loud to no one. He might not let himself touch, but there was no fucking rule of his that said he couldn't watch.

Several jack and cokes later, Athena and Sabine were well on their way to being trashed at Teddy's, a local bar not far from the hospital. So far they'd turned away numerous advances and free drinks. Sabine said it was like picking apples, you never just went for the first one; you inspected the crop and then chose the one that would taste the sweetest.

Athena was glad they were taking some time away from the hospital to really sit down and talk, although they saw each other almost twenty-four hours a day, they never had much of a chance to really spend quality time together. She missed her friend.

"So the surgery with Mills, it went well?" Athena asked, referring to one of the pediatric attendings.

"Yeah, it really did. I finally got my first cut and I think I'm really starting to like Peds. It might be where I end up as my specialty," Sabine revealed.

The two had been friends since college, and then moved on to the same medical school. Each not having much family, they'd relied on scholarships and grants to get through the programs. Sabine had been an orphan since the age of fourteen, bumped around through the system and it was a miracle she turned out as well as she did. Athena's mother had died at a young age, she didn't have many memories of her at all, and the ones she did have were fuzzy. Her father had passed away a few years earlier from cancer; a loss that hit her hard. She missed him terribly and wished every day that he was still alive to see her accomplishments.

"I think Clarence has a little sparkle in his eye for you. Don't let Cian catch wind of that," Sabine teased, knocking back another drink.

"What? Clarence? Don't be ridiculous. We're friends."

"Oh, you're friends; but he wants to be the type of friend that you don't wear your panties around."

"What is your obsession with my panties!"

"What? You're hot, Thene. If I was into girls, I'd do ya in a heartbeat."

"You've lost your damn mind," Athena laughed and then stood to make her way to the ladies' room. The drinks had hit her a bit harder than she thought and she wobbled on her feet as she weaved her way through the crowd of people. After taking care of her business, she came out of the stall and peered at herself in the mirror as she washed her hands. Her olive eyes had a bit of glazed look to them and her head full of curls, courtesy of Sabine, was tousled. She looked carefree and relaxed, two things she hadn't felt in a long time. Getting out was a perfect idea, Sabine as usual, was right. Not that she'd ever admit it, of course.

When she stepped out of the bathroom, she collided hard with a body and immediately apologized as she put a hand out to steady herself. Strong arms came around her and she looked up into the face of a very handsome man with warm brown eyes and a soft smile.

"The fault is mine, gorgeous. Although I can't be angry with myself for bumping into someone as beautiful as you." His voice was smooth and his lines even smoother and Athena found herself considering if this man could be the one that got possession of her panties that night. *Ugh, Sabine is starting to rub off on me.*

Before she could reply, her pager went off her in small black clutch. In the distance, she thought she heard another one and realized it must be Sabine's. Taking it out, she saw it was an emergency page to the ER. *Great, I'm drunk and there's a trauma coming in.*

"I'm sorry," she told the stranger. "I'd love to stay and chat more but I have to go. Raincheck?" She didn't wait for an answer, just slipped out of his arms and tottered her way back to Sabine who was already flagging down the bartender to pay their tab.

"We—"

"I know we have to go, trauma coming in," Sabine interrupted her before she could explain. They quickly settled the bill and then hurried outside to try and hail a cab. The line of people waiting for one was enormous and neither of them would get very far on their high heels after the amount of drinks they'd had if they tried to walk back to hospital.

"Excuse me," Athena called to the bouncer. "We're doctors over at Lincoln Hospital and we need to get there right away. Is there any chance you could help us out with a cab? It's an emergency."

The large dark-skinned bouncer looked them over from head to toe and laughed in their face. "Sure, you're doctors'. And I'm Ryan Seacrest." He turned his back on them and continued checking ID's.

"No, you don't understand—"

"I'll take you." Athena froze at the sound of that voice. The voice she would know anywhere. Spinning, sure enough, there was Cian standing a few feet away, hands in the pockets of his black dress pants, white shirt unbuttoned a bit at the collar. He looked casual and sexy and her traitorous mouth watered at the sight of him.

"What are you doing here?" she demanded, her tone coming out harsher than intended. The shock of seeing him again outside the hospital had butterflies dancing in her stomach and her skin tingling with anticipation. She wanted to order him to explain himself right that second, she wanted to leap into his arms and kiss him senseless like that day in the on-call room, she wanted to turn and run in the opposite direction as fast as her stilettos would carry her. The damn man was slowly driving her insane.

"Well seeing as it's a bar, I was here having a drink," he answered dryly. She flushed and looked down at her feet. Of course, he wasn't following her. She was the dumbest person alive for even considering such a thing.

"Oh. Right, of course," she mumbled, looking to Sabine for help. It wasn't necessary though as Cian just continued on.

"Look, if you're coming, we need to go now. The pile-up on the highway was bad, multiple casualties and injuries from what I can gather. You two lushes will have to get an IV until you're sober, but you can observe until then." The girls nodded and followed Cian down the street to where his Jag was parked.

"Wait! You really are doctors?" the bouncer called after them.

"Don't quit your day job there, Ryan! They sure are lucky to have you," Sabine yelled back, flipping him the bird.

They laughed and even Cian cracked a rare smile at her joke. The ride to the hospital was short and when they got there, Cian disappeared ordering them to report to Webster for instructions.

"Jesus, look at you two," Webster sighed when they wandered over to where she was handing out assignments to Oscar, Bianca, Dick and Clarence. "Of course its two of mine that are the messes."

They hung their head sheepishly and muttered out, "I'm sorry's."

"Well, never mind. I don't have time to deal with you two right now. Clarence, go with them and get them on IV's. Then get your ass back here, we're going to need all hands on deck now that we're two interns short. You two, I don't want to see you again until that alcohol is out of your system. Understood?"

"Understood." They answered in unison and followed Clarence. After changing into their scrubs, he sat them both down in a free bay and got started on their IV's.

"Where the hell did you two go? And where the hell was my invite?" he asked, looking put out.

"Sorry, Clarence. This was girl's night out. We just needed to blow off a little steam." Athena told him, feeling guilty for leaving him out.

"Well next time, I'm coming with you. You're not the only one that could use a break from this place once in a while." He looked Athena right in the eye when making his admission. She shared a look with Sabine who mouthed "I told you so," earning her a glare to shut up from Athena.

"Sure. We'll pick a night after work and go grab a couple drinks all of us together," Athena told him with a smile. She was starting to get a pounding headache, an after affect that she always suffered from when drinking, and was about to ask Clarence to get her some aspirin when she spotted Seth Holloway headed their way.

"Seth?" she looked at him, surprised to see him back at the ER so soon. He'd been making a habit of dropping in occasionally to check on her which she thought was so kind of him, but he'd only been there a few days earlier so to see him back again was a surprise.

"Hey, Athena. What happened? Are you alright?" he rushed forward the last few steps after seeing the IV in her arm and placed a hand on her head.

"Oh, I'm fine. Just had a few too many at the bar and trying to get sober so that we can be of some help in the ER," she was embarrassed to admit the reason she was bagged, but didn't want him to worry it was something serious.

"Well, that's a relief. You had me worried for a second there, gorgeous." Athena blushed and wanted the floor to open up and swallow her when Clarence and Sabine just stared at the both of them, wide-eyed.

"I need to get some statements from a few of the victims that were brought here. This crash on the highway is one hell of a fucking mess," he explained, dropping his hand from her hair and stepping back. "I'd love to talk more with you though. I'll find you before I leave, okay?"

"Okay, sure. That sounds great," she told him and gave him a warm smile. Seth left and Clarence followed, banging his utensils in his basin and pushing the curtain aside roughly out of his way.

"You. Little. Whore. Three! Three men all obsessed with you! Jesus fuck, Athena. It's like a goddamn three ring circus around here. I can't get enough," Sabine burst out as soon as they were alone.

"What? Shut up. No one is obsessed! Seth is just concerned about me after the attack is all and Clarence is our friend—you know that. And Cian, well Cian is in an entirely different league. I have no idea what his deal is."

"Sure. Keep telling yourself that. God, this just keeps getting better and better." Sabine was all but bouncing with excitement.

Finished with getting their IV's, they wheeled themselves to an unoccupied corner of the department and watched as the ER came to life as patients were rushed in and out and doctors worked to repair damage and save lives. Looking around, Athena spotted Clarence eyeing her with a look of sadness as he worked to clean debris from a woman's arm; Seth shooting her a cocky smile as he raised an eyebrow and then winked at her; and Cian consulting on a major trauma just brought in but watching her with a burning intensity that just about set her skin on fire.

It was going to be a long night.

chapter twelve

"GOD, WASN'T THAT amazing?" Bianca exclaimed as she and Athena exited the OR. They had scrubbed in together on a neurosurgery that had blown both their minds. The surgeon, Dr. Gamble was attempting to remove a tumor in the patients' brain without affecting any of their motor skills. The size of the tumor is what made it a complicated procedure, but Gamble was known to be one of the best in the field and she'd knocked it out of the park. Now they just had to wait and see if the patient still had the use of all of her speech and motor skills when she awoke.

"It was. What a rush, I've never seen an exposed brain before," she admitted. Over the past few days, Bianca had been making more of an effort to connect with her, Sabine and the other interns. She'd been opening up about herself and sharing her dreams of what she wanted for her career as a surgeon. She was the first in her family to graduate high school, let alone becoming a doctor. Shyly, she'd shared how proud she was of herself for not only finishing school, but being accepted into the surgical intern program at Lincoln Hospital. No one in her family had ever done anything remotely close to that before and she hoped to set an example of what they could do if they just applied themselves and put in the hard work.

"She let me dissect some of the tumor even! Can you believe that?" Bianca still wasn't over that shock. Usually Athena got chosen for all the awesome opportunities in surgery but this time, it was her and she was on cloud nine about it.

"You earned it, you studied and knew that procedure inside out. It was amazing to see you shine in there, Bianca." Athena told her sincerely. While she would have loved the experience for herself, she recognized that she was given a lot of breaks and special privileges from the residents and attendings'. It felt good to see it happening for someone else.

They joined the other interns in the locker room, still talking excitedly about the surgery. Dick was changing into his street clothes, Sabine was engrossed in sending a text message, Oscar was his usual quiet self and Clarence grinned at them as they came through the door.

"Oh, look, if it isn't the Wonder Twins," Dick snarled at them, in a particularly nasty mood. The rumor of the day was that he'd received a tongue lashing from the trauma attending for his poor bedside manner and being unprepared. He wasn't progressing in the program as quickly as the other interns and his lack of skill was showing with each passing day. There'd been a few weeks there where he'd actually showed promise of being a decent guy, but lately he'd reverted to the same asshole they'd met on the first day.

"Wonder Twins?" Athena repeated, not sure what he was getting at.

"You two think you're hot shit, coming in here bragging about your big surgery, flaunting it in all of our faces." He spread his arms wide to encompass the room. "Especially you, Athena." He pointed at her and took a few steps closer. "You're nothing but a fucking whore who spreads her legs for anyone to get ahead in this game." He was directly in front of her now, seething.

Athena was shocked into silence and just stared at him, unable to form words.

"And don't give me that fucking wide-eyed innocent look. You may have them fooled," he motioned to the other interns again. "But you'll never fool me. I see you for what you really are. A no-good piece of fucking trash that doesn't belong here. Unless of course, you're willing to give me a piece too just like you were that junkie in the lab? How far'd you let it get with him, huh? I bet—"

He didn't finish his sentence as to everyone's shock, Oscar pulled him away from her and punched him square in the nose.

Blood spurted everywhere, spraying Athena's face and shirt and Dick cried out in pain, clutching his broken nose and doubling over.

"Don't speak to a lady like that," was all Oscar said before opening the door to the locker room and walking out.

In the meantime, Sabine had come to her feet and stood in front of Dick where he was still moaning and crying out, "My nose!"

"You're lucky that Oscar beat me to it, you limp dick, shit for brains douche. If it were me, you wouldn't be walking right now, let alone crying your eyes out about your damn broken nose. Let me spell it out for you, Dick, you're jealous. Jealous of all of us because deep down inside you know you don't belong here. You'll never be half the doctor Athena or any one of us is and you're sure as fuck never gonna get in her panties. So why don't you do us all a favor and go play in traffic for a while?" Sabine was furious and didn't hold back her temper over his treatment of her best friend.

Dick glared at all of them and then turned and fled out the door. Athena didn't realize she'd been crying until Sabine came to her side and handed her a tissue. The things he'd said...yes, she understood he'd said them only to hurt her and attempt to drag her down into the misery he was feeling, but there was some truth to his accusations as well. Everyone did gossip about her and why she got the opportunities she did. It was something that she despised and having it thrown in her face in front of her peers was a huge burden to shoulder.

Clarence started towards her but she raised a hand to hold him back. "I need a minute, guys. I'll see you all tomorrow. Sabine, thank you." She walked into the bathroom and shut the door, locking it and leaning her head against the wood frame. Shame filled her and she had a hard time forcing it back down. There was no time for self-pity. She'd put herself in a mess with Cian and it was up to her to get out of it. She just had to figure out how.

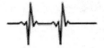

Bianca left work later than the rest of the interns after spending time in the research lab pouring over articles and textbook chapters on heart transplants. She knew the whole team was counting on a heart being found for little Sebastian in the coming weeks and when that happened, she wanted to be the best prepared intern to scrub in on the surgery. After her shifts were finished, she liked to leave the hospital through the basement and walk along the side of the building to the bus station. There was a set of train tracks that ran parallel to the hospital and she enjoyed watching the cars chug by while waiting for her bus home.

This part of the hospital was usually deserted and she liked to think that she'd discovered a well-kept secret. A place she could come on her breaks to be alone and think; a nice escape from the madness of intern life. Lately, she'd realized that by segregating herself from the group, she was starting to become invisible. And invisible meant never picked for surgeries which didn't fit with her goals. She'd been making more of an effort to fit in and actually found herself enjoying spending time with the others, with the exception of Dick, of course. That guy was a complete jerk and she hoped he sunk his own ship sooner rather than later.

Rounding the last corner before the exit, she heard low voices and stopped. Curious, she crept forward, being careful to remain quiet as she strained her ears.

"I know, Reynolds. This new schedule actually is working in our favor. After we killed that last guy, Alan Hilliard, I'm more convinced than ever that we should try to convince the Chief to leave us all on this rotation. It's much easier to dispose of these fucks at the beginning of shift than it is in the middle or the end." Bianca covered her mouth when she heard the name of a patient that had died on the table a few weeks prior. Was that Dr. O'Reilly? What did he mean they'd killed him?

"Yeah, I've got the next one lined up. A real fucking winner. This woman is a child pornographer. Yeah, another one. We'll get her taken care of at the end of the month. Then after that, I want to talk to you about tracking down those two serial killers. I think we can do it. I'd love to get them on my table and hear them scream until they're fucking dead."

Bianca stumbled back, shocked and in her haste, backed into a shelf of supplies, sending a few metal buckets crashing to the ground. Horrified at the explosive noise she'd made, she turned and ran, desperate to get away before she was caught eavesdropping. She heard Cian chasing after her and pumped her legs harder, frantic to get away. Seeing an exit, she burst through the door and dashed across the parking lot and into the field, headed for the train tracks. She was fast, always had been and knew if she could make it there, she could lose him on the other side.

Fuck, he was a killer! Thoughts raced through her mind as she ran and she remembered a news report about a vigilante somehow protecting the city from criminals that had escaped punishment for their crimes. Was he the vigilante? What would he do if he caught her now that she knew his secret? Chancing a look back, she saw that he was only a few feet behind her and gaining ground.

"Bianca! Stop, wait! Come back here!" he yelled after her. She refused to listen and kept running, intent on getting as far away from him as possible until she had time to figure out the truth about what was going on. Reaching the chain-link fence, she thankfully found a hole small enough for her to wiggle through and climbed under, confident that he wouldn't be able to fit. She kept going and raced towards the tracks, looking behind her to see him climbing up the fence, trying to avoid being cut on the old barbed wire.

Panicked, she turned back but lost her footing and fell hard onto the tracks, bashing her head off the ground. She momentarily saw stars and her vision swam in front of her. There was a loud buzzing in her ears and she was dimly aware of someone yelling her name but she couldn't make sense of the words. Looking up, she saw Cian racing towards her from several yards away, waving his arms like a madman.

Confused, she looked up and saw the train barreling down on her at top speed. She screamed and tried to get up, but found her pant leg had got caught in the tracks, trapping her. Wiggling, her movement sluggish due to the pain in her head, she tried to get free but it was no use. Cian was screaming her name, the train was inches away and all she could do was close her eyes.

"Nooooooo!" Cian bellowed just as he reached the tracks and the train hit her. He was seconds too late and she was obliterated by the force of the train; a sickening sound echoing around him. Sinking to his knees, his head dropped to his chest and he pulled at his hair with both hands. What the fuck had she been doing in the basement? He wasn't going to hurt her, only explain and hope that she could understand that the work they were doing was vital; important. Now, it was too late and a young life had been cut short unnecessarily. Guilt washed over him and his head spun with a gut-wrenching sense of shame. He may not have pushed her onto those tracks but he was responsible nonetheless.

Bianca Sullivan was dead and her blood was on his hands. How he was going to explain this to Reynolds and the others he didn't know, but he knew he had to make himself scarce before the train operator called it in and the police arrived to investigate what happened. Her death was a tragedy, but it couldn't get in the way of the higher purpose he served; to rid the streets of New York of the ruthless criminals that escaped the punishment they deserved.

chapter thirteen

THE NEWS OF Bianca's death rocked the hospital. Athena was playing cards with Sebastian early one morning before finishing a night shift rotation when Sabine came to the door, her complexion gray and her eyes glazed over. Instantly concerned, she ruffled Sebastian's hair, which was getting thinner by the day, and told him she'd be back to see him the following afternoon. He nodded and gave her a brave smile, trying not to show his disappointment. Feeling her heart crack a little, she pulled a baseball card from her pocket and slid it across the bedside table for him.

"Ellsbury!" he cried out. "My favorite player, thank you, Athena!" This time his smile lit up his whole face and warmed Athena's heart. She really did love that little boy.

Following Sabine out into the hall, she reached out and rubbed her arm, concerned about what was going on that had her best friend so distraught.

"What is it? What happened, Sab?"

"Bianca's dead." she said it simply, no leading up to it, just a one-two punch that hit Athena right in the gut.

"Wh—what? Dead? What do you mean she's dead? I just saw her yesterday." Tears sprang to her eyes and spilled over, as she fought to understand what Sabine was telling her.

"They found her...on the train tracks."

Horror filled her and she covered her mouth to keep from being sick. "Oh, God no. Sabine, tell me that's not true."

"I wish I could, Thene. I don't know all the details but the rumors say she was stuck. The operator saw her trying to get free to run, but..."

"Stop. I can't. Oh, Jesus fuck, no." Images of Bianca trying to get herself free to run flashed across her face and had her heart dropping down to her stomach. The sheer torture she must have felt, the panic to try and get free before the train...

"Athena." She turned at the sound of someone calling her name and spotted Seth standing a few feet away. She immediately rushed over to him, hoping for a miracle.

"Tell me it's not true, Seth, please. It can't be true."

"I wish I could do that, but I can't. We confirmed that the remains are hers. I'm so sorry, I know she was your friend." He cupped her face in his hand and rubbed his thumb lightly across her cheek, catching one of her tears.

"What happens now?" she asked.

"Well, I needed to get a few statements to find out why she was still here so late, but it's an open and shut case as far as we're concerned. The operator states she was stuck on the tracks, trying to get away. We confirmed his story with the evidence that was left behind." He didn't go into it any further, wanting to spare her the graphic details. "This is just a senseless tragedy. I wish I had more to tell you, to offer you some comfort, but all I can say is that you should know that she didn't suffer. It would have been very quick." Athena nodded, grateful for what little information he gave her. It was still a shock, but it helped some knowing that she didn't suffer.

"Listen, I've got to get going. There's been another abduction and Babbs and I split up to cover both cases."

"Another abduction? But I thought those killers left town," Sabine said.

"We thought so as well, but this is the same MO as the previous abductions. We're concerned after the...outcome of the last kidnappings." Seth sighed and rubbed a hand down his face. For the first time, Athena noticed how haggard he looked and her heart went out to him. Working as a detective in New York City couldn't have been an easy job, not with the rising crime rate.

"Let me know if you need anything," she told him sincerely. "And thank you, for the information about Bianca."

He squeezed her hand and then left them, promising to get in touch later that week. She locked arms with Sabine and they headed to the locker room, intent on finding Webster and the others. When they entered, Clarence, Dick and Oscar were all there and Webster was seated with them on one of the wooden benches. Dick's eyes were bruised and his nose had a thin strip of white tape across it from where he'd been hit by Oscar.

The room was filled with a somber silence. No one needed to say a word to know that they were all affected the same way by the news of Bianca. Shock and sadness hung in the air like a black cloud, clinging to each of them. After several moments, Webster finally spoke.

"Bian—" her voice broke and she took a steadying breath. "Bianca was a wonderful girl with a bright future in surgery. What happened to her was a tragedy and no matter what I say, it's not going to make it hurt any less. All we can do now is keep pushing forward. She had a love for this program and we can honor her by continuing to do what she no longer has the luxury of doing—be surgeons."

The locker room door opened again and Chief Murphy stepped in, followed by Cian. Both had grim looks on their faces as the took in the group of interns.

"By now I'm sure you've all heard what happened to Bianca. This is a terrible loss and I want you to know that I've arranged for grief counsellors to be brought in and be available to talk with you, should you feel the need to do so. I've been in touch with her family and once we know the arrangements, you'll be free to attend the service; we all will. From what I know, this was possibly an accident, but police are still investigating." Chief Murphy informed them.

"It was ruled an accident," Athena blurted out. All eyes turned to her and she fought to keep her voice even as she clarified.

"Se—Detective Holloway was here. He let us know that it was in fact an accident as far as their department is concerned."

Cian's stare burned into her when she mentioned Seth's name and if she didn't know any better, she would have thought he was jealous. The Chief nodded and then asked them if they had any questions. When everyone mumbled no, he waved Webster out into the hall with him and left with Cian.

The five of them stared at each other, not sure what to say. Finally, after several long, uncomfortable moments, Athena broke the ice.

"She was amazing. I'm definitely going to miss her and I know you all will too. What we need to do now is focus on the future. Dick, it's time you stop being such an asshole to all of us. You don't have to be our best friend, but we certainly deserve to be treated with respect."

Dick nodded and for once didn't comeback with a smartass remark.

"You're right, Athena. We need to stick together and remember what we're here for. To become the best surgeons we can be," Clarence spoke up.

"Agreed," Sabine said, offering him a slow smile. No matter what they said in the locker room, or what was said out in the hallways, the fact of the matter was that they'd lost one of their own. Bianca was dead and nothing about that was right. Nothing about their lives in the hospital would ever be the same.

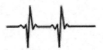

Towards the end of her shift, Athena was walking down the hall after checking on her last patient of the day, a young woman who'd suffered a bad fall and needed orthopedic surgery to repair a nasty break on her left leg. She'd be immobile for a few weeks but she was in good spirits about it which helped to lift Athena's melancholy mood.

She let out a muffled yelp when a hand darted out and she was dragged into an on-call room, the door slamming shut and locking behind her. Her heart leaped into her throat and she dragged in the breath to let out a scream for help.

"It's me, Athena." *Oh, Cian.*

"Oh, my God, you nearly gave me a heart attack!" she swatted him on the arm and paced away, furious at him for scaring her. "What do you want?"

"I wanted to make sure you were okay. To have a few minutes to talk to you in private. I'm truly sorry about your friend, Athena. I mean that," his eyes searched hers, looking for some sort of validation that she accepted his apology as sincere.

"Thank you, Dr. O'Reilly. That really means a lot." She smiled at him and then turned to leave, startled when he grabbed her by the arm and spun her, pushing her up against the door.

"Don't go." he whispered and lowered his nose to her ear, breathing in her scent, his breath sending a wave a tingles down her spine. He took one hand and stretched it out above her head, pinning it to the door and locking their fingers together.

"Cian," she breathed, knowing that she should push him away, but instead arching her back and thrusting her breasts into his chest, needing to feel more of a connection to him.

"I want to spend some time with you. Take you on a date," he whispered as he let his mouth fall to her lips. He gently tugged her bottom lip between his teeth and bit down lightly, darting his tongue out to trace her upper lip. She sighed and he took advantage and slipped his tongue into her mouth, in and out over and over he made love to her mouth until she was panting beneath him and starting to grind her hips into his.

"Have dinner with me tomorrow night." He placed light kisses from her lips to her ear and then ran his hand down the length of her arm to caress her breast through her top.

"Okay," she agreed, against every instinct screaming at her that it was a bad idea. But no matter how much she knew it was a mistake, a larger part of her argued that it wasn't. That being in his arms was where she was meant to be. The darkness that she saw in him, it called to the light that lived in her. They fit together as though they belonged. She wanted to see what else he kept hidden from the outside world. What other parts of him were carefully concealed under the facade he had firmly in place. She should probably be terrified of what she might discover but instead she was excited, enthralled and ready to experience anything he would share with her.

His lips smashed back to hers and this time his kiss was anything but soft and exploring. It was hard and demanding, brutal and erotic. His body was pressed so close to hers it was as though they were one and she couldn't wait to feel him when he was pressing he down into her mattress, driving his cock into her over and over again.

Pulling back, he looked her dead in the eye, delighting in the way she looked completely disoriented; his lips rosy from his attention.

"Tomorrow. Dinner, seven p.m., your place. I'll bring the wine." He gently moved her aside and then opened the door and left without another word, leaving Athena staring after him wondering what in hell just happened.

chapter fourteen

THE PASTA SAUCE was simmering in the pan and the fresh bread had just been popped in the over to melt the cheese on her homemade garlic bread. Pasta was her favorite meal and she hoped that Cian wouldn't mind something as simple as that for their date. It wasn't often that she had a chance to spend any time in the kitchen due to her busy schedule, most nights she just made a peanut butter sandwich for dinner or grabbed something quick on the drive home, so getting a chance to cook—she wanted to make one of her favorites.

She'd lived in her apartment for four years and absolutely loved it. It was a modest size with two bedrooms and one bathroom; the perfect amount of space just for her. When she'd first moved in, she'd thought about getting a cat or a small dog to help combat the loneliness, but quickly realized that it wouldn't be fair to an animal as she wouldn't be home enough to give him or her the love and attention it deserved.

Her cell rang and she knew without even looking at it that it'd be Sabine. She'd called seven times in the last hour, barking orders on how to style her hair, to pick up fresh flowers for the table, how to apply the perfect smoky eye for her make-up. She was furious that she had to work and couldn't be over there bossing her around on how to get ready for her date.

Athena hit the speaker button on the phone to answer the call. "Yes, dear." she teased, knowing it would drive Sabine nuts.

"Don't dear me. Okay, you've got less than thirty minutes before he gets there and Cian doesn't strike me as the kind of man that's late to things. In the bathroom, in the second drawer behind the eye mask pads is a bottle of vanilla scented body lotion. Use it. Everywhere. And don't argue," she added as Athena opened her mouth to do just that. "Next, break out that sexy black lace set that I know you have from Victoria's Secret. It's subtle and perfect for under your dress."

"Dress? But I was just going to wear—"

"Yeah, I know. You were just going to wear some stuffy dress shirt and pants and look like it was time to be interviewed for a position in HR instead of dressing to impress and have him imagining what positions he's going to be lucky enough to get you in tonight. You're wearing the black one with the lace cut-out back. I wanted you in the white, but knowing you, you'll spill your damn dinner all over it."

"Since when did you get so bossy? And mean?" Athena moved to the bathroom and opening the second drawer, found the body lotion and yanked the top off to give it a sniff. It smelled good she grudgingly admitted to herself.

"You'd be a mess without me and you damn well know it."

Athena rolled her eyes, but deep down she knew Sabine was right. She'd been a nervous wreck ever since she'd come out of her desire-filled fog and realized that she'd agreed to a date with Cian. A date for God's sake. With a man she wasn't even sure she liked no less.

"You're right, Sab. I really wish you were here. Am I an idiot to be doing this?" She lathered her hands up with the lotion and began to apply it. Its sweet aroma filled her nostrils and she had to admit it was pleasant.

"No. Thene, you two have been doing this dance for months. With all the shit that's happened, you deserve a little mindless fun. Just relax and don't overthink things."

"But you've heard about his reputation just the same as I have," she voiced her main concern about letting Cian in as she entered her bedroom and pulled out the black lace set that she saved for special occasions. Pitifully, those had been few and far between lately as she tried to remember the last time she'd had a need to wear sexy lingerie. At least a year. Jesus.

"His reputation is for exactly the opposite of this. He never dates. Or chases, or is even nice to women. He's interested, Athena. You owe it to yourself to see what could be. If not for you, then dammit for me. I need details! That man is sexy as fuck and I'm not the only one that's totally jealous of you."

"I just don't need any more gossip than I already have." She rooted through her closet until she pulled out the dress that Sabine had instructed her to wear, taking a second to admire it. It had been a rare find at a department store several months ago. As soon as she'd spotted it, she knew it was meant to be hers. As she slid the material over her head, she again marveled at the way it fit her like a glove; hugging her trim waste and accentuating her high breasts without being over-the-top slutty. The cut-out back with the hint of lace gave it that subtle sex appeal and the material whispered over her skin where it ended just above her knee. She sent a silent prayer of thanks to whoever it was that invented side zippers as she pulled the clasp closed.

"Don't forget the heels. The red ones, not those ugly black flats." Sabine's voice called out from the bed where she'd tossed the phone.

Athena frowned. She *liked* her flats. But she obeyed and dug out the red ones out to slip her feet into. Finished, she moved her closet door to take a look in the full-length mirror.

"Fluff up your hair a bit. You're lucky enough that you get that sexy, tousled look without having to work for it like the rest of us. Bitch." Athena laughed and ran her hands through her long, dark hair, giving her head a tiny shake to have the locks falling back into place.

"What about—"

"No jewelry. It's only going to get in the way later." The woman was a damn mind-reader. There was a knock at the door and her heart skipped a beat. That would be Cian. And ten minutes early just as Sabine predicted.

"Oh, God, he's here. This is a mistake. I can't do this. What was I thinking?"

"Stop. Relax, you got this. Just hang up the phone and go and open the door...it'll all fall into place from there. I promise. And if he fucks up, don't worry, I'm ready to kick his ass. Have fun, love you, Thene."

"Love you too. Thank you, Sab."

"Yeah, yeah, all you people would be lost without me." She disconnected the call on Athena's laugh.

She took a deep breath and pulled the door open, pleased to see him dressed semi-casually in a fitted dress shirt and a pair of dark jeans. He held a bottle of red wine and a slow, sexy, smile passed over his face as he looked her up and down.

"Hi," she said shyly and opened the door to let him in.

"Hi, back. You look gorgeous," he told her as he stepped inside and kissed her cheek. She sighed and she closed the door behind him.

"Thank you." She took the wine and headed into the kitchen to check on dinner. "Make yourself at home and I'll pour us a glass."

Cian roamed around her small living area, checking out her space. He'd been there once before but hadn't taken the time to really look at the place. Unlike his apartment, pieces of Athena were everywhere. Framed photographs of her and Sabine covered almost every surface and there was even one of the six interns, likely from their first day since Bianca was in it. His heart twisted seeing her face and the guilt at what had happened to her started to rise up again. He shoved it aside, reminding himself for the millionth time that he'd tried to get to her in time. He was inadvertently at fault, but her death was more a tragic accident.

"Is this you and your father?" he called out to her, picking up a framed photo of her and an older man in front of a Christmas tree. Their arms were wrapped around each other and their smiles were full of love.

"Where?" She poked her head out of the side of the kitchen and seeing him with the frame, nodded. "Yes. That's the last Christmas we spent together before he passed away."

"I'm sorry," he told her as she carried out the two glasses of wine, handing one to him. A sad smile crossed her face as she took the photo from him and looked down at it.

"Thank you. I still can't believe he's gone. I've caught myself hundreds of times going to pick up the phone to call and share something with him. It makes the pain fresh all over again every time I realize that I can't."

"I understand," he mumbled, taking a sip of her wine. She had no idea how completely he knew how she felt. Placing the frame back on her small end table, she smiled.

"Anyway, enough of this sad talk. Dinner is just about ready if you want to sit down? I hope you like pasta."

What he liked, was watching her ass as she walked back into the kitchen. The sway of her hips was gentle and the dress stretched just perfectly across it. His hands itched to grab that little ass and lift her up and onto his cock, feel her tight body pressed against him as he kissed her senseless and filled her over and over with powerful thrusts until she was screaming out his name and begging for more.

"—recipe. It's my favorite." He came back to the moment just as she was carrying a large steaming bowl of pasta and a plate of freshly baked bread into the dining room, setting them on the table beside a large serving spoon. "There's just something about this one that I love, I hope you like the way everything tastes." She glanced up at him and smiled. Even in her sexy as fuck red heels she still towered over her by a few inches. She went to move back into the kitchen to grab a few more napkins just as he went to move to take his seat and that was it. Their bodies collided and the spark was electric. The second their skin connected he could no longer resist and he snatched her into his arms, feeding off the look of shocked surprise in her olive eyes.

His mouth claimed hers in a kiss that seared her down to her soul as his hands encircled her waist and lifted her up, sitting her on the dining room table and leaning down to deepen the kiss. Her hands found their way into his dark hair as she pulled him impossibly closer, desperate for more. His tongue swept inside to find hers and they dueled in a battle for control as she moaned. The more of him he gave her, the more she wanted to discover, until she'd unlocked every secret he was hiding.

The harder she fought the attraction, the more her body ached to feel his touch. He had the power to make her lose all self-control. And she liked it. Liked the way he made her feel. He dragged his mouth away from hers and picked her up off the table, wrapping his arms around his waist as he headed in the direction of the bedrooms.

"Which one?" he asked against her mouth.

"There," she gestured with her head and he kicked the door open heading straight for her king-sized bed. Dropping her down, he trailed his hands down her smooth legs to remove her shoes, smirking when her body trembled at his feather-light touch.

Moving back up her body, he found the zipper on the side and slowly tugged it down, then watched as she shyly pulled the dress up and over her head. Her long dark hair fell back around her shoulders, covering her perfect breasts in a sexy display. He growled and leaned in, lowering his head and teasing a nipple through the delicate lace of her bra.

"Fuck, Athena. You smell amazing and you're so fucking delicious." Cian reached around behind her and unhooked her bra letting it fall down her arms, baring her to him. Her breasts were full with pink hued nipples that he couldn't resist. He tweaked one between his thumb and forefinger, rolling and tugging while he sucked the other into his mouth, licking her ever so gently. She arched into him as he switched and repeated the same on the other side. The little sounds she was making in the back of her throat were driving him fucking crazy.

Athena could barely stand it and if he kept it up, he was going to make her cum from just his attention on her tits. Her fingers found the buttons on his shirt and made quick work of ridding him of it, her hands traveling over his six-pack headed for the V that made her mouth water. Unbuckling his belt, she slipped her hand into his boxers and found him hard and pulsing. His cock was long and thick and her pussy definitely took notice as she felt dampness pool between her legs as she wrapped her hand around him and began to stroke him in a slow manner.

He groaned and not moving his mouth from her nipple cupped her aching pussy through her panties.

"Soaked, baby. I fucking love that," he mumbled and trailed hot kisses down her stomach, circling her belly button with his tongue before stopping at her panty line. Not wanting to go slow any longer, he pushed them aside and used two fingers to spread her juices as he rubbed up and over her clit and then sinking them deep inside. She gasped and he moaned as he filled her to the knuckle. She was tight and hot and felt so fucking good. She was already starting to clamp down on his fingers; he increased the speed until he was fucking her with his hand, feeling her build closer and closer.

She brought her head closer to his and his mouth captured hers just as she climaxed, her scream getting lost in their kiss.

He pulled back to watch her head fall back and the rosy glow spread over her body. She was fucking magnificent. The monster living in his veins screamed to devour her. The man he wanted to be fought to protect her. Regardless what side of him prevailed, the truth was clear. She was his for the taking.

He pushed his boxers the rest of the way down his legs and she got an eyeful of him in all his naked glory. He was hard, lean muscle and without thinking, she ran her tongue up and over this toned abs, wanting to taste him. He knelt between her legs and lifting them over his shoulders, speared her with his tongue as he lapped at her pussy, letting his mouth roam over her in a slow, leisurely exploration that sent her spiraling towards her next orgasm. He speared her with his tongue and continued to drive her closer and closer to the edge and when she finally exploded, he moaned; the taste of her was so damn intoxicating and sweet.

"Condom?" he asked, not sure how much longer he could hold back from sinking balls deep into her. She gestured at the bedside table and he plucked one out and rolled it on.

"You're so fucking sexy, baby. I fucking love watching you come apart for me. Your greedy little pussy wants more doesn't it?" His dirty talk had her blushing but he was right; she wanted his cock in her so bad.

"I need to feel you, Cian. All of you," their eyes locked and again the chemistry sizzled. Unable to wait any longer, he sank into her slowly, giving her time to adjust to his size as he stretched and filled her.

"Fuck, you're tight," he groaned as her wet heat latched onto him, pulling him deeper. He set a rhythm that was slow and meant to give her time to get used to the feel of him but she was having none of that as she bucked her hips to meet him thrust for thrust, forcing him to drive into her deeper.

It wasn't long before he could feel the familiar sensation building inside him. Wanting to bring her to another climax, he reached between their bodies and found her hard little nub, pinching and twisting it. When he felt her tighten around him again and yell out, "Cian!" he let himself go and pushed stream after stream of his release into her, grunting out her name as he collapsed on top of her.

Rolling to his side, he got up to discard the condom. Coming back, he did something he hadn't let himself do in a very long time. He let himself relax and drawing her into the circle of his arms, he enjoyed the feel of her warm body next to his. Their hearts raced in unison and for a moment, he felt content.

"So much for dinner, huh?" she joked and his shout of laughter surprised both of them.

"Don't worry, Payne. I won't leave here tonight until I know you're fully satisfied."

chapter fifteen

AFTER THEIR DATE, Cian and Athena didn't see much of each other for a few days due to busy schedules on both their parts. He'd snuck out in the wee hours of the night, after making love to her three more times and binging on re-heated pasta with her in bed. Her laugh, her smile, every tiny thing about her was starting to affect him. When she'd finally fallen asleep, he'd slipped from her bed and left a note saying he didn't want to wake her.

On the drive home, the guilt started to set in as he thought back over what they'd done. What would Hannah think? How could he do something so intimate with Athena? Something he'd last shared with only his wife. Shame and self-loathing washed over him. What kind of man was he that he was enjoying life with another woman while his wife rotted in the ground because he hadn't been able to save her? As much as he knew it was going to hurt Athena, he needed to cut all contact with her to strictly professional. He'd let his emotions get in the way after Bianca's death and that was on him. Athena was a pure soul who deserved someone that would be able to walk with her in the light, not lurk in the dark like him.

He didn't have time to mull over how he was going to break her heart as his next target was emerging from the gas station a few miles away from the hospital. He mentally reviewed the information he'd collected on her in his portfolio:

Marian Seely, age 41
752 Main Street, Queens
Accused of child pornography, child molestation, accessary to sexual assault of a minor,
suspected in the death of at least one child

Case was brought to trial, but thrown out due to evidence being lost and/or tampered
with.

A mistrial was filed and Marian was set free

The information of the mistrial boiled Cian's blood. Someone screwed up at the lab and all physical evidence was mistakenly discarded, leaving them with nothing to tie her to the crimes. She was guilty as fucking sin and everyone knew it, but without a conviction, she walked free as a bird.

He watched her get in her car and then walked over and rapped on her window, making sure to keep the needle in his hand hidden.

She rolled down the window and let her brown eyes travel down his body. "Well, hello, handsome. What can I do for you?" Her attempt to flirt with him churned his stomach. She was attractive, but given what she did for her extra-curricular activities, he'd rather bite his own cock off than let it near a cunt like her.

"Hi, yourself. Listen, my GPS quit in my Jag—" he motioned to his sleek silver car parked at the pump behind him, watching her eyes light up at the sight of it. "Any way you can give me directions? I'm not from around here." He flashed her a dazzling grin to back up his lie.

"Those foreign cars aren't all they're cracked up to be, huh?" she smirked at him and it took everything in him not to smash her face off the steering wheel. "Let me get my phone and I'll see if I can look up directions to where you need to be. Maybe you'll have time for a cup of coffee before you get back on the road?" She raised a brow at him, letting him know coffee was not what she was interested in.

"Maybe I will," he winked at her and wanted to punch himself in the face, but needed to play along. She turned her body to reach for her purse and quick as a snake, he reached out and inserted the needle into her neck.

"Ouch! What the f—" Her body immediately went into convulsions as the drugs worked through her bloodstream.

He pulled out his phone and dialed 911, shouting for help and grinning with glee on the inside.

Thirty minutes later, the team was assembled and ready in the OR. After he'd scrubbed, he snapped on his gloves and picked up a new tool. An eight-inch long knife that he'd been dying to use on one of his patients. With what Marian had gotten away with, she was the perfect candidate for what he had planned.

The need in him grew with each breath he took.

Inhale. Stalk forward.

Exhale. Grip the knife.

His eyes narrowed on his prey and sharpened, piercing through Marian's squirming form on the table. The hunger consuming him took form, morphing into a viable force.

Inhale. Flash a cold grin.

Exhale. "The price for your sins must be paid," he told her, looking her dead in the eye and watching as the fear grew when she saw the knife.

"Marian, Marian. You seemed like such a nice lady back at the gas station. Tell me, what is it that possessed you to abuse children the way you did? To put them on display for all the sick fucks out there that get off on that kind of shit? Was there really no other way for you to make a fast buck?"

She didn't answer him of course, she couldn't with her mouth being gagged. "Or maybe, you got off on it too and that's why you did it. Either way, it stops here. You stop here. This is where I'm ending you and making sure no one falls victim to you again."

He raised the knife and brought it down across her skin lightly at first and then harder, carving into her. The blade was smooth and cut through her like she was butter. The blood sprang to the surface pooling and then running over as she bucked from the pain.

After a few minutes of playing with his new toy, he tired of it and ordered his scalpel. Slicing her open he used a retractor to spread her open and peered down at her heart.

"Ah, there's your heart. Do you know, hearts are my specialty in the OR. I save lives in here and I'm damn good at what I do. Isn't that right, Reynolds?"

"Yes, sir. You're the best of the best."

Cian grinned. "You hear that, Marian? I'm the best of the best. So that's why I know that when I do this..." he wrapped his hand around her heart in a crushing grip. "That it will hurt like no pain you've ever felt before."

Marian screamed behind her gag and tears flowed freely down her cheeks and she gurgled and tried to beg for mercy.

"And when I do this," he punctured a hole in her artery. "You're going to bleed out in exactly five minutes. So it was nice knowing you, Marian. Boy am I glad I never have to see you again and the poor innocent children who's lives I just saved will be happy too—from afar of course."

When it was over, he left the OR whistling. His mind was focused. His conscience was clear. But his hands...those were stained with the blood of his prey.

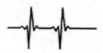

Athena had been unsure what to think after she woke up the morning after her date with Cian and he was gone. He did leave a note which Sabine said made him not a total jackass, but their conversations and interactions had been limited since then and had her wondering if she'd made a huge error in judgement when she jumped into bed with him.

Deciding to take the stairs up to Sebastian's room instead of the elevator, she opened the door and promptly collided with someone.

"Oh, I'm so sorry!" she exclaimed without looking up. "I was lost in thought and didn't see you..."

"It's okay, Payne." *Cian.* Her head snapped up and their eyes clashed together, each surprised to see the other. Despite herself, her pussy sat up and took notice as he smelled so damn good and she'd missed him. He was obviously having a similar reaction to seeing her as he dragged her into the stairwell and pushed her up against the wall. He didn't speak, just claimed her lips in a way that branded her to him and then let his hand dive into her scrub pants, moaning when he felt how soaked she already was for him.

Her hands went to the string at his pants and he shoved hers down and before she knew it, her legs were around his waist and he was slamming his cock into her.

"Fuck me," he breathed as he set a brutal pace. This wasn't about love making. This was fucking. Hard, primal, and full of passion. Their eyes never left each other as he sank deeper with each powerful thrust. Their fingers locked together and she bit down hard on her lower lip to keep from crying out. Her head fell back against the wall as she had two rapid-fire orgasms in a row, grateful when Cian's mouth landed on hers to capture her cries.

When he was close, he let her down, pushing her shoulders to get her to sink to her knees. She understood what he wanted and immediately opened her mouth for him to push in and continue fucking her face. She tasted him, herself and her own release; the pure eroticism of it had her pleasuring herself with her own fingers to reach one more climax just as he shot his down the back of her throat.

They stared at each other panting hard as they came down from the high of their release. Cian looked down at her with her face flushed and her hair tousled, her lips swollen from his attention. All he wanted to do was pull her to her feet and tell her how fantastic she was. That he was starting to fall for her. Instead, he did the opposite.

"Our dealings need to remain strictly professional after this. This was inappropriate, Dr. Payne. You crossed the line here. I won't take this out on you in the OR, as it was a good time for me too. But it won't happen again."

Blown away by his words, she fell back on her heels, embarrassment and shame staining her cheeks a deep red. "Cian? I don't understand. I thought we were building something here. I thought—I thought that—"

He cut her off before she could say the words that would break his resolve. "You thought wrong. You should have paid better attention to the rumors about me, Dr. Payne." With that, he left her sitting in the stairwell; turning his back on the one woman that might have been able to show him some semblance of happiness again.

"That motherfucking cocksucker said what?" Sabine was furious after finding Athena sitting alone in the locker room after having a shower. She'd needed to wash away the evidence on her skin of what she'd done with Cian in the stairwell.

"It's over, Sabine. He played me and I fell for it hook, line and sinker. I'm nothing but a fool."

"You shut the fuck up right now. You're not a fool. He's a goddamn moron and if he thinks he's going to get away with this, he better think again." She rose to her feet but Athena reached out and took her hand.

"Please. Just leave it alone. This is going to be humiliating enough for me once the rumors start and I just can't take any more drama." Her tone was defeated and her eyes were downcast. She'd really thought she'd been falling for him, and him for her. What a joke.

"Fine. But just for now. If I went after him now I'm liable to kill him." Athena smiled gratefully, she was so lucky to have Sabine, a true loyal friend that always looked out for her.

They left the locker room and headed for the cafeteria, Sabine insisting she'd feel a bit better after eating something.

"Okay, I'm sorry, but in the stairwell? Damn girl, that is so hot! Since when did I become jealous of your sex life?" Athena smiled and although the hurt was still fresh, the fact remained that it was the hottest sex she'd ever had in her life.

"Well you can rest assured that things will now revert to normal. I'll go back to being the boring one and you can have all the fun." She stopped dead in her tracks when she spotted Cian at the end of the hall, flirting with one of the young nurses.

Hurt speared through her that he was already moving on to his next conquest. She really had been an idiot to think that there was something other than a manwhore to get to know about Cian O'Reilly. Steeling her spine, she prepared herself to walk past them.

"Athena!" her name was shouted from behind them. They both turned and coming down the hall was Seth. He looked handsome as always in a fitted gray t-shirt and a pair of jeans.

"Seth? What are you doing here?" It was obviously his day off since he wasn't wearing his badge.

He flashed her a smile as he came to a stop in front of them. "I'm here to see if I can steal you away for an early dinner."

"Dinner? You mean like a date?" she was surprised, but not shocked as she thought he might be interested in her like Sabine had been saying all along.

"Yes. Like a date. Just keep it casual, I know this great burger place over on 42nd."

She looked at Sabine who was nodding and glaring at her, meaning that she better say yes or there'd be hell to pay. Glancing down the hall, she saw Cian twirl a lock of the nurse's hair and her stomach revolted in disgust.

"I'd love to. But can we make it tomorrow night? Today has been a bit of a rough one, I don't want my mind clouded with other things."

"You got it. Tomorrow it is. It's a date."

She smiled at him but it didn't reach her eyes. Cian met her gaze and his jaw locked. "Yes. it's a date."

chapter sixteen

MARCUS AND DANE had been laying low for weeks after Layla escaped and almost blew everything for them. Thankfully, Dr. Daniels had a place set up for them to flee to after they'd taken care of the witnesses. Dane was beyond livid that they'd had to dispose of the girls they'd collected in one fell swoop, Marcus had wasted precious time reasoning with him that there was no way to take the girls with them without attracting unwanted attention. In the end, it was Dane that had killed them all, his rage taking over and butchering them before Marcus could get him out of there. In that moment, he saw Dane's mother, Mila in him. Pure evil radiated from him; sinister and depraved, he was worse than Mila in many ways. His devious side was not to be reckoned with. Even Marcus, who was no saint, feared Dane a little bit and the things he was capable of. Attempting to rein him in had proved unsuccessful so far and he feared it always would be.

His thoughts drifted to his long-lost sister, Emma, and how her boyfriend, Sam, still was putting up roadblocks in him getting to know her. After revealing himself to her several months earlier, he'd expected her to welcome him with open arms; to want to get to know who he was. He was her true family after all. However, that was clearly not the case and instead they'd involved that fucker from his past, Gabe Thornton, who was intent on tracking him down and seeking retribution for what he did to him and his wife, Nora. He hadn't expected that reaction from Sam since he'd worked so closely with Mila for such a long time. People always surprise you at what they can hide.

Dane's blood lust appetite was growing with leaps and bounds every day. They had a new girl picked out and they were setting plans in motion to take her that evening. That would bring them up to two and Dr. Daniels was pleased as well since he wanted to run some tests on them. It still burned his ass that he lost so much of his research back in Norton Springs when their black market ring had been shut down. He'd been slowly collecting data again ever since.

Descending the stairs into the sound-proof basement of the condo they were staying in, he called out to Dane.

"Dane? Are you down here?" A whimpering cry answered him and he guessed that he was as their guest seemed to be in some discomfort. When he rounded the corner, he found her suspended from the ceiling with her bound hands extended above her head, thrashing back and forth as Dane used his small razor blade to slice at her milk-white skin.

The girl was covered in marks; her skin was starting to actually look more red than white. She was rail thin but her ribs were much more prominent now than when she first arrived. He made a mental note to ask Dane if he'd been remembering to feed the poor girl.

"Finish up. We need to go over the plan one more time before we set off. And take a shower before we go. You need to clean up."

Dane whipped his head around and his gaze burned into him in anger at being told what to do.

"I'll handle it. I'll meet you upstairs in five." The girl's eyes pleaded with Marcus to help her, but if she thought he was the good guy in this scenario; she was sadly mistaken. He wasn't the good guy; there was no one to save her. There was no one to save any of their souls from the depths of hell they'd descended into.

Since they had more time to plan, Seth took her to a little Italian place that was cozy and intimate. She'd almost backed out of their date, recognizing that she'd only agreed in an irrational plan of making Cian jealous. When she'd got home and had time to think, she realized it wasn't fair to do that to Seth, who genuinely was a really great guy. Sabine had intercepted her before she could pull out however, so there she sat in a cute yellow sundress while Seth told her a little about himself.

"Well, I didn't grow up in New York, and I never wanted to be a cop. It was always my father's dream for me to follow in his footsteps. I wanted to do something a little more; something that would really help me leave my mark behind in this world, you know? It wasn't until there was a spree of robberies in my hometown that helped me to see there was more to being a cop than just paperwork and long hours. You were given the opportunity to help people; to solve crimes. After that, I took my dad's advice and here we are now."

"I'm sure he's very proud of you," Athena said, accepting the glass of red wine the waiter poured for her. They ordered their meal, lasagna for Seth and spaghetti and meatballs for Athena and then settled back into their easy conversation.

"I've always dreamed of being a surgeon. I played doctor with all the other kids when I was young and it just stuck. The human body fascinated me and I wanted to learn more. Getting the internship at Lincoln is like a dream come true. I just didn't know it would come with all this heartache."

Seth reached across the table and took her hand in his, squeezing her fingers. "I know that attack must still haunt you, and then Bianca's death...I can't imagine how that felt."

Athena felt a horrible amount of guilt as she wasn't referring to either of those things; she was referring to Cian and the way he'd played her for a fool. Seth mistook her expression for grief over her friend, and brought her hand up to kiss her knuckles.

"Tell you what. After dinner, I'll take you to one of the best secluded rooftops in the city. It's got an amazing view and we can just spend some time together alone. Talk about anything you want." It did sound wonderful, but again Cian flashed into her mind and that infuriated her. Would she always be haunted by him and the mistake she'd made?

"I'd like that," she forced out and then pushed her chair back. "Would you excuse me for just a minute? I need to go to the ladies' room."

"Of course."

She escaped into the ladies' room, sighing in relief when there was no one else in the stalls. Splashing cold water on her face, she stared at herself in the mirror hating how much Cian was affecting her.

"You're an idiot, Athena. Cian doesn't want you. You need to get over it."

"Well, I wouldn't say he doesn't want you exactly. That's not the issue at all." Jumping at the sound of a voice behind her, she spun around and came nose to chest with Cian...in the ladies' room.

"What? What the...How did you get in here?" she demanded, trying to slip past him. He gripped her by the upper arms and sat her on the sink, trapping her in place with his powerful thighs.

"I used the door," he answered dryly, holding her struggling body in place.

"Well use it to get the fuck out! You're not allowed in here!" She sounded like a four-year-old child telling someone what toys they couldn't play with. He looked so damn sexy dressed all in black, his hair still a bit damp from a recent shower and his scent invading her nostrils due to his closeness.

"You don't want me to get out, Athena. Just like you don't want anything to do with that numbskull detective other than friendship. What you want—is me." His voice was low and husky, causing hot need to coil low in her belly.

"No. No, I don't want you. You're an ass. You're mean and cruel and you just used me to get what you wanted and then left me on the floor like some cheap whore." To her horror, her eyes started to sting with tears and she blinked furiously to hold them back. She'd be damned if she cried any more tears over this man.

Seeing her fight for control was too much for Cian to bear. He thought he could walk away from her, that it was best if she forgot all about him. But when he saw her with that damn detective and he had his hands all over her, all rational thought went out the window. All that mattered was making her see how sorry he was and that he wanted another chance.

"I fucked up. I shouldn't have treated you that way and I'm sorry, Athena." He mustered all the sincerity he could into his voice, hoping she'd see how much he meant it.

"Well you're too late, I'm with Seth now. He's a real man and he knows exactly how he should and shouldn't treat a lady. And he's dynamite in bed. So you see, I'm just fine without you. There's nothing you have that I need."

Cian's brows snapped together in anger at her words. He pushed his hand up under her dress and felt how damp with need her panties were. She involuntarily arched at his touch and he instantly grew hard, loving how responsive she was to his touch. Shoving her panties aside, he coated his fingers with her wetness and then brought them up to push into her mouth. She sucked them against her better judgement, unable to stop herself.

"You taste that, baby? That's your arousal, that's your *need* and it sure as hell isn't for old Seth out there. It's *mine*." She glared at him, furious that he was right and that he'd moved his hand when all she wanted was to feel him shove them inside her and make her cum.

The tension crackled between them, each battling a war with the other. Him wanting her to submit and admit she wanted him, her wanting him to chase her and show her how much he wanted her. Unable to take it anymore, they moved in unison until their lips smashed together. Athena moaned at the contact, it'd only been a day but she already missed him so much. He dragged her closer across the sink until their bodies were aligned and every curve of her matched the curve of him. His hands found their way under her dress again and her drew her panties down, plunging two fingers into her aching pussy; driving in and out over and over until he pushed her so far over the edge she saw stars.

Sheer force of will was the only thing that kept her from screaming out his name as he drove her up towards the peak again, his mouth moving from her lips to nip at her ear. "You feel that, baby? I'm what you need. Not him, not anyone else. *Me.* Only I can make you come apart like this, when you close your eyes, it's me you think of, not Detective Do-Gooder out there. You want me as bad as I want you. Admit it and I'll give you what you want. Tell me it's my cock you want to feel right now and it's yours. Just say the words, Athena."

Her head lolled on her shoulder and she moaned as he bit down on her neck. "I—I..." she paused and looked deep in his eyes. How could she give him the words when she couldn't trust him to say them back? "I have to go," she burst out and pushing him back, she jumped down from the sink, straightened her clothes and rushed out the door.

Back in the restaurant, she quickly made her apologies to Seth, telling him she wasn't feeling well and fled out the front door before either man could catch her. She was so fucking screwed it wasn't funny. She needed to get away, fast, to collect her thoughts and figure out what the fuck she was going to do.

chapter seventeen

"WE HAVE WONDERFUL news, Mara," Cian told Mrs. Harris one morning a few weeks after his forbidden rendezvous in the bathroom with Athena on her date with Seth. Mrs. Harris looked up from the crossword puzzle she was doing while Sebastian slept, hope coming alive in her eyes.

"You don't mean...?" her voice was a whisper so as to not wake Sebastian, who had been sleeping more and more frequently lately.

"I do mean. We've got a heart, we just got the call a few minutes ago and I've scheduled the surgery for this afternoon."

Webster and her interns were in the room as well since they'd been on the case since the beginning. One intern would be lucky enough to be chosen to scrub in and Athena was wishing like hell that it was her. Not because of what she was to Cian—who knew what that even was anyway—but because of what Sebastian meant to her and what scrubbing in on a transplant surgery would mean for her career. There would be a specialized team in the OR for this procedure seeing as it was a pediatric surgery as well as a cardio one. They'd likely even open the galley for spectators to view and take notes.

"That soon? Wow, I need to call—" Mara's mouth formed an O of horror as she realized what she was about to say. Athena knew immediately what had happened. Her knee-jerk reaction was to call her husband for support, but she could no longer to that.

Athena moved to her side and took her hand. "Who do you need here? We can call them for you, Mrs. Harris."

Mrs. Harris smiled at her gratefully. "It's just my sister out in Ohio. She won't be able to make it, but I'd like her to know it's happening today."

"I'll get her information from the nurse and take care of it," Athena promised.

Despite their best efforts to keep their voices low, all the chatter in the room roused Sebastian from his slumber. He opened his blue eyes slowly and looked around at all the faces staring at him.

"That's a lot of people first thing in the morning," he said in such an earnest tone that the whole room burst into laughter. Mrs. Harris leaned over him, and stroked his hair back from his forehead.

"Sebastian, honey. All these people are here to tell us some very good news," she told him softly.

His eyes sought out Cian and then Athena. "Athena, I don't think I'm going to be able to play cards today, you'll have to find something else to do."

His sweet voice and his brave attempt to make jokes broke every heart in the room while they all fell simultaneously in love with him. For a four-year-old boy that had been cooped up in a hospital for as many months as he had to still have his optimism and sunny outlook on life, it was inspirational.

"That's okay, Sebastian. I'd much rather you go and get your brand new heart today. We can play cards tomorrow. I'll even let you beat me." She winked at him.

"I always beat you!" he exclaimed, although for him it was more like a loud whisper. His breathing had been getting worse and worse over the last few days. "Are you going to be in the surgery, Athena?"

She paused unsure what to say. Of course she wanted to be in there desperately, but the call wasn't hers to make; it was Cian's. Avoiding eye contact with everyone, she held his hand and squeezed.

"We'll see, little man. And if not, don't worry. I'll be right here waiting for you when you come out."

"She'll be in there too, buddy." Cian announced causing surprised looks from everyone, Webster included. After giving Mara a few instructions for Sebastian's activity that day, the doctors filed out, having got their assignments from Webster. Sabine and Athena were headed to the ER for the day, Oscar and Clarence both had post-op rounds on patients and Dick was assigned to general surgery as their case load was heavy.

Sabine was silent the entire walk to the ER which was completely unlike her. Confused, Athena touched her arm to get her to stop, bewildered when she pulled away.

"I just need a minute away from you right now, Thene." she told her, her tone flat.

"What? Why? What's wrong?"

"What's wrong? What's wrong? I'll tell you what's wrong. Why does every fucking thing have to be about you all the damn time? Maybe some of us studied their asses off for that surgery too so that they could have a shot to scrub in. Maybe some of us have things in our personal lives that could use some attention now and then or a shoulder to lean on. You're so focused on Dr. Dark & Mysterious that you've forgotten you're not the only fucking intern in this hospital and you sure as hell aren't the only one with problems! Just because you're sleeping with your boss, none of us get seen and I'm getting really sick and tired of it. I earned my spot here just as much as you did." Without another word, she turned and left Athena standing in the hallway completely flabbergasted at her outburst.

People whispered and stared and pointed as she walked by. Sabine's yelling had been heard by everyone and her face burned in embarrassment. Thankfully, Smith took pity on her and sent her into Bay 1 with a patient that needed sutures so she could hide from the prying eyes and low whispers.

"Hi, I'm Dr. Payne. I'll be sewing up your arm today," she said to the teenage girl laying on the gurney.

"You're the doctor that just got yelled at by that other doctor. I saw. Boy, she really let you have it," she commented. Athena frowned at her but didn't say anything.

"When I'm mad at my best friend, I just send her a text message with the mad face emoji. Yours...wow she really is pissed at you."

"I know. I know she is, okay? Can we not talk about this? What happened to your arm?" she asked, changing the subject. She already knew from reviewing the chart, but needed to distract the inquisitive girl.

"Oh my friend dared me that I wouldn't cut my arm with a swiss army knife. She lost. She doesn't believe how tough I am."

"That's not tough, that's stupid. You could have really done some serious nerve damage."

"Well you're stupid for not realizing that your friend needed you."

"I'm not stupid, she didn't tell me she had things going on."

"You're her best friend, you should have known."

"Yeah, well your best friend should have known that you could have really hurt yourself with this stunt. Don't do something like this again."

"Don't be so self-involved next time that you forget who your friends are."

The two stared at each other for a few minutes, before having to grudgingly admit that the other had a point.

"Fine," they said at the same time.

"Now shut up and let me get these stitches in so you can go home."

Athena spent the rest of the morning and part of the afternoon seeing patients that came into the ER. Sabine glared at her every chance she got and each time she felt worse and worse. She needed to get her alone so that they could hash everything out.

Her pager went off and it was time to head to Sebastian's room to get him prepped for surgery. They'd both been called and the walk to his room was a stony one. Unable to stand the tension, she tried to reach out.

"Sab I—"

"Don't, Thene. Not here. We'll do this after work." Athena frowned. So it was okay for her to scream at her in front of everyone at work, but not for her to try to set things right. Sighing, she let it go.

Sebastian kept up the chatter as they got him ready and Mrs. Harris hovered, unsure what to do with herself. Once it was time to wheel him away she burst into tears and threw herself on top of him.

"Oh, God, Sebastian, Mommy loves you so much. My brave, brave boy. Daddy loves you too and he'd be so proud of you if he was here. You be strong in there and I'll be right here when you come out."

"Don't worry, Mom. I got this. Grand slam! I love you too!" he called out as they started to wheel him out the door. Athena looked back at Mrs. Harris as she all but collapsed in the chair, her body wracked with sobs and knew what she had to do.

"Sab," she motioned her forward. "Go with Sebastian. I'm staying here."

"What? No, Thene. If this is about what I—"

"It's not. It's just the right thing to do. Go and scrub in, you can do this, I know you can. There's no one else I trust more. I need to be here with Mrs. Harris."

Together they watched until they could no longer see them down the hall and then began the torturous act of waiting.

Several hours later, Mrs. Harris finally spoke, having sat quietly for most of the time. "Jay and I were high school sweethearts. We got married right after we graduated which pissed off both of our parents'," she said with a chuckle. "He went into trade work so that I could go to college and get my degree to become a teacher. He was always putting my needs above his."

Athena reached out and took her hand, recognizing that she needed to talk.

"I found out I was pregnant on the first day of my new job as a teacher. We were counting on me working for a few years before we started a family so that we could get caught up on some bills and create a little nest egg for ourselves. I remember being so scared to tell him, afraid that he might leave me." She took a deep breath before continuing.

"When I finally did tell him, you know what he did? He took an ad out in the paper to announce that we were expecting. He worked three jobs during my mat leave so that we could make ends meet. He was the best man I've ever met." Tears rolled down both their faces now as she shared her very personal memories with Athena.

"It sounds like he loved you very much, Mrs. Harris."

"Please, call me, Mara. We're sharing one of the worst experiences of my life together after all."

She smiled and nodded. "Okay, Mara. I'd like that."

"When we found out Sebastian was sick, I got the news first. I called him in a panic, bawling my eyes out. He was so worried about me, about us, that he rushed home. Rushed so bad that he got in that car wreck and he died. He died, Athena, and it's all my fault," she buried her head in her shoulder and let all the grief flow out of her. The months and months of stress worrying if her son was going to be alright. The all-consuming loss over losing the love of her life; all of it. It all came out in those tears that now soaked through Athena's shirt.

"No, Mara. No. It's not your fault. It was a horrible, tragic accident. Do you think that Jay would have wanted to be anywhere else once you got that news? No, of course not. He loved you, he loved Sebastian and he just wanted to be there for you. To be with his family."

"What am I going to do if I lose both of them, Athena?"

She didn't get to respond as at that moment, Cian and Sabine rounded the corner, headed their way. One look at Cian's face and the dried tears on Sabine's face and she knew. Dread filled her, sadness enveloped her and all she wanted to do was hold Mara forever to spare her the pain that was inevitably coming her way.

The tears started to fall silently and she could literally feel her heart crack in two. Sebastian's little face swam in front of her. The light in his blue eyes as they played cards, his excitement when his team won. They way he liked to tell jokes. It wasn't fucking fair. He was just a child.

"Mara." Cian called her name. She pulled out of Athena's arms and glanced up, seeing them there and freezing. Like Athena, she took one look at their faces and knew.

"No." she whispered. And then she screamed it. "Nooooo! My baby! Not my baby boy, please God, no, no, no. Sebastian!" Her wails grew louder and Athena couldn't keep it together as she grabbed her and wrapped her in her arms.

"No! You promised! You said if we got a heart he would be okay. That it would fix him. You promised!" she raged at Cian, pinning him with a hateful glare. "My son...oh, God, Jay not our son too."

"I said it was our best chance for him, Mara. He was very sick and we wanted to give him every opportunity we could to come out of this. I—" his voice cracked, an unusual occurrence for him. "I wanted him to come out of this."

Looking up at him, she saw how he too was devastated by the news. Saw the doctor that had been by her son's side day in and day out for months, working to find solutions to better his health. All the anger drained from her body and just her grief remained. She launched herself into his arms and sobbed into his chest.

"H—H—He was only f—f—four years old. He never got to live. My baby, oh, God. No, Sebastian." Cian led her away to have a private moment, leaving Athena alone with Sabine. As soon as they were out of earshot, she too let her tears fall, sobbing over the loss of such a precious little boy with so much love to give.

Sabine stepped forward and they embraced, the comfort they both needed trumping the fight they'd had.

"Thene, about what I said..."

"It's okay. You were right about most of what you said. I should have been there for you to lean on. You sure as hell could have picked a better venue for your little outburst, but I understand where you're coming from."

Sabine looked embarrassed but before they could get into it any further Athena told her she wanted to check on Mara, see what they could do for her. Sebastian's death was a large lead rock sitting in her chest. She couldn't believe such a sweet boy had been taken so young and yet assholes like those two serial killers were still walking around. Life really wasn't fucking fair.

chapter eighteen

CIAN HAD BEEN filled with rage ever since losing
Sebastian on the table. That little boy had looked up to him;
trusted him to get it right and he'd failed him just like he'd failed
Hannah. Waiting for the twenty-third day had been torture as he
needed some sort of an outlet to channel all his pent up fury. He'd
been taking things slow with Athena, the death had hit them both
hard and they needed time to process their feelings. Plus, that
fucking Detective was still hanging around and that was really
starting to piss him off. She was off the market, claimed, taken, *his*.
They may not have made anything official, but he shouldn't have to
tell her that he was not a man that shared nicely with others.

He was sitting in the living room watching the news, before
leaving to pick up his target and heading into work. Mornings were
his thing, he liked to drink his coffee and peruse the paper and
news channels for more criminals to add to his portfolio. He looked
up as that idiot, Rae Kelley came on screen.

"Good morning! I'm Rae Kelley, here with your morning
update from Channel 15. New York City is still baffled by our
reports of *The Watcher*. Is he friend or foe? The body count keeps
rising, but suspiciously each victim linked to him is a hardened
criminal that escaped prosecution. If I were someone thinking
about going on a crime spree in this city, I'd beware. You just never
know if *The Watcher* will end up with you in his sights! Be sure to
tune in daily to Channel 15 for updates on this developing story
and check out my blog, *Rae's Ramblings* for up to the minute news."

Cian swore and switched the TV off. He'd thought the
vigilante reports had died down, but obviously he was wrong. The
more media attention that stayed on this, the more difficult it was

going to be to keep it going. He'd have to sit down at some point and think up a strategy to get the heat off him and his team.

Downing his last sip of coffee, he headed out the door to pick up his newest patient. His dark excitement to get this fucker on his table put an extra spring in his step as he walked to his car.

Damien Lock, age 36
59 West 32nd, Upper West Side
Accused of date rape, serial rape, murder, attempted murder, assault and battery
Witnesses failed to testify, insufficient evidence to convict

Damien Lock was one cold-hearted son-of-a-bitch. He had a real, deep-seeded hate for females and it showed in every one of his victims. He'd brutally rape and beat them repeatedly, either leaving them battered beyond recognition or he just killed them altogether. A wealthy corporate type, he thought he was untouchable. Until he messed with the wrong victim who reported his ass. After that, women started coming out of the woodwork, telling their stories. Unfortunately, as fast as they appeared, they disappeared, some never to be heard from again. It was obvious he was having them silenced, but with no proof, there was nothing the authorities could do. In the end, like so many other criminals, he'd walked. But now came the time for him to pay the price. His price; his way.

Getting him to the hospital was going to be tricky since he was a corporate executive, but with some creative genius, he was able to set up a lunch meeting at a high-end restaurant with a fictitious client looking to invest in the company. That got Damien alone, which was exactly what Cian needed. While seated at the table, Cian walked by and casually dropped a tablet into his Damien's glass of water and then kept right on moving. It dissolved instantly and it didn't take long for the commotion to start as he collapsed onto the floor in convulsions.

As soon as the ambulance was called, he rushed off to the hospital to arrive before it, thus avoiding any suspicion. He couldn't have been more thrilled with how smoothly it had gone. His one and only hiccup was Athena. She materialized from nowhere, hinting around that she'd like to scrub in on a surgery to start off her day. He tried to dodge her and pretend that he didn't catch her meaning but he wasn't sure if she bought it. In the end, he managed to wheel Damien away and leave Athena behind, but he knew he'd have major damage control to do later.

In the OR, he could barely contain his excitement to try out his new toy. Liquid nitrogen was set up and ready for use. His plan was to inject it into Damien and ultimately freeze him alive while he worked on him. When everything was set, he stepped up to the table to begin.

Sixteen needles. Sixteen needles sunk softly into the flesh of the offending man. He moved to the side and reached across and pressed his thumbs over two of the ends of the needles.

He met the eyes of Damien, delighting in the terror reflected back at him. The drug would be injected into his system in three...two...one...

He knew exactly the second it hit his bloodstream as Damien's entire body went stiff and his eyes widened even more if possible. "Saw," he ordered. Once it was in his hands he leaned over so that Damien could get a good look.

"So, Mr. Lock, I hear that you like to torture innocent women. Rape them, beat them, even murder the unlucky ones. Then when they finally decide to make you pay for your despicable acts, you have them wiped out! Well, that's rather ungentlemanly of you, don't you think?"

Damien could only blink, his eyes were the only part of his body that weren't completely frozen solid.

"I think you need to be punished, Mr. Lock. Fair is fair after all, and lucky for me, I'm very good at what I do."

He walked to the end of the table and looked at his feet. "Hmm, wonder how fast you'll be able to evade the law without these?" He lowered the saw, but instead of cutting off the entire foot; he started with a toe. It clattered to the table and he picked it up to examine it. "Fascinating. No blood at all. No muss, no fuss, torture. I like it."

He removed two more toes before walking back up to Damien's side. Damien's eyes were scooting all around the room, desperate to see what was happening since he couldn't feel a thing.

"Curious to see more, are you? Let's see what we can do about that." Using a scalpel, he obtained from Lorna, he set to work removing one of Damien's eyes partway from it's socket. The only indication that he felt anything at all was the bugging out of his left that was still intact while he worked on the right.

The sick monster inside him had been released, the longer he tortured Damien, the farther he wanted to push himself past the point of no redemption. The rage he still felt over Sebastian's death, Hannah's death, his role in Bianca's death—it was starting to eat away at the last good parts of his soul that were left. It wouldn't be long before his facade of being a respected professional was erased and the killer that he was destined to be was all that was left.

Disgusted with himself and finished with Damien, he gave the order to remove the liquid nitrogen. He'd already cut the main artery, so once he was thawed, he'd bleed out like all the rest. He'd feel every injury first though and that was what Cian wanted the most. To have him suffer the way he'd made his victims suffer.

Turning to leave the OR, he ran smack into Athena who was just coming in.

"Oomph," she said as they collided. "Oh, good they sent me to get you. There's a case in the ER that needs you right away. Hey, do they need help in there while you go? I can stay." She craned her neck to see around him and took in the scene. "Is that guy alright? What happened to him?"

Cian grabbed her arm and dragged her away as quickly as possible before she could see anything else and put things together.

"He's fine. Reynolds is just waking him up now. Why don't you go see what they need from me in the ER. Tell them I gave permission for you to take my report and I'll be right there."

Athena frowned at him, but obeyed, not wanting to do anything to upset him. As she walked away, she replayed what she saw. The man looked frozen? And what was with that saw and no other medical staff in the surgery with him besides two nurses and Dr. Reynolds? Something wasn't right and all her instincts were screaming at her to leave it alone. Of course, she didn't want to do that and likely wouldn't until she got to the bottom of what she saw.

Ever since Sebastian had passed away, Cian had been distant with her. Gone was the man who was dangerously attracted to her, and in his place was one that was cold and closed off. He still treated her with respect and the sex was still mind-blowing; but there was something missing. A piece of him died in that OR as well, a vital piece that she feverishly wanted to help him get back. She had a feeling that without it, he would sink farther into the darkness she knew was within him and this time, he may never find his way back.

Arriving in the ER, she found Seth waiting for her, a bouquet of roses and a picnic basket in his hands. He looked handsome and hopeful and she truly hated herself for what she was about to do. He was such a kind man and she couldn't continue to string him along when her heart was somewhere else. He deserved better than that.

"Hi," she greeted him warmly, accepting the kiss on the cheek he gave her. "What's all this?"

"I wanted to surprise you since our last date didn't turn out as planned. Thought maybe you could sneak away for half an hour—not off hospital grounds—and we could share some lunch together."

He really was so sweet and adorable. She truly wished she felt more for him than friendship, but the fact was that she didn't. A romance between them wasn't meant to be. He might have been the better choice, he definitely was the safer choice; but he wasn't her heart's choice and that's what she had to follow.

"This is so wonderful of you, really. But I really can't sneak away today, I'm sorry. We're slammed in the ER as you can see, and I promised Sabine I'd have lunch with her if we get a break since things have been a little rocky between us."

Disappointment fluttered across his face and Athena felt like scum. Here he was trying to do something nice for her and she was weaseling out of it with a lame excuse.

"Seth. I have to be honest with you. I don't see this going anywhere more than a friendship. I think you're a wonderful, kind man, but I don't have any feelings for you that way and it isn't fair to you for me to pretend that I do." She tried to step forward to touch his arm, but he backed away.

"It's that doctor, isn't it? O'Reilly? He's the one you're hung up on?"

"It's a lot of things, Seth. Starting with the fact that I'm an intern and my time is barely my own. I'm not ready for anything right now except practicing medicine and becoming the best surgeon I can be."

"Yeah. Well good luck with that." Hurt was all over his features as he turned and walked away, pausing to dump the roses in the trash.

Feeling like an asshole, she headed to the trauma room to let them know Cian would be right down and to see if she could help.

"You know; you did the right thing." She turned to see Dick standing there, obviously having observed the scene with Seth.

"I know I did," she replied, unsure where he was going with the conversation.

"He'll be pissed for awhile, but he'll get over it. Good to see that maybe you aren't just spreading your legs for everyone, Payne." With that parting comment, he left her standing there, confused if he'd insulted or complimented her. She shrugged it off, she had bigger things to worry about—like just what in the hell Cian was doing in that OR.

chapter nineteen

"PLEASE, PLEASE LET me go home!" The girl's terrified screams and pleas for help were the first thing Marcus heard when he opened the door to the basement and walked down the stairs. They had five captives now that he was aware of, Dane sure had been busy. Dr. Daniels was in his element, giddy and eager every time a new girl arrived at the house that he could run tests on. He was determined to re-start the black market ring they'd lost several years earlier. Marcus couldn't blame him; it had been a very lucrative time for them indeed.

He, however, had different priorities. Such as getting to know his sister and avoiding that annoying Gabe Thornton who seemed intent on finding him to exact some kind of justice. So far, they'd been able to evade him as he was acting alone and didn't have the best tracking skills. Still, it was a worry they needed to keep an eye on, just to be safe.

Dane was working over the newest girl in the corner of the basement. She was exposed from the waist up and her long, beautiful chestnut colored hair was in a messy array around her face. Dane had made several gashes up her legs and was now starting to focus on her midsection, ignoring her screams and cries for him to stop.

"Dane. We need to talk," he told him and without waiting for a reply, headed back up the stairs, ignoring the girls held in captivity. Dane was getting out of control with his abductions. His work was sloppy and it was only a matter of time before he got them caught. Marcus Drake was not a man that did jail. It was time he knocked some sense into Dane once and for all.

"What is it?" Dane asked as he came upstairs, rubbing his hands together to spread the blood. Marcus motioned for him to take a seat at the kitchen table.

"You need to scale it way back. You're getting far too fucking careless and you're going to get us all caught if you're not more careful."

"What the fuck are you talking about? I'm careful. I'm not the one who's been caught before by the way, that's you. Like three times if I remember correctly."

"That's not the point. The point is that you're pissed off and it's starting to show in your work. So either smarten up, or get the fuck out."

Dane sat back as though Marcus has slapped him. Get out? Where the fuck was he supposed to go? Marcus knew what he was. He knew what was inside of him and how he had to feed the craving for blood. Hell, he'd made him! Sold his soul to the devil and ruined any chance he would have ever had at a normal life.

"You're a fucking asshole. You're just like me, if not worse, and I'm the one that has to get back in line. Un-fucking-believable."

"We were lucky we got away after that fucking disaster with Layla. Do you really want things to get that close again? To have the cops breathing down our necks and everything we've done and are planning to do be exposed? Use your fucking head, Dane."

Dane sat there seething, furious that Marcus was treating him like an insubordinate instead of a partner. They were in this together, he had no right bossing him around and telling him how to run things. If he fucking wanted to take ten girls at once, that's what he'd fucking do.

Shoving away from the table he got to his feet. "If you're done lecturing me, I'm going out."

"Fine. Go. But mark my words, Dane. If you don't start using some fucking sense, you're going to bring this all crashing down on us. Again."

Dane slammed the door to the house without saying a word. Getting in his car, he backed out of the driveway and tore off down the road, driving aimlessly. He was keyed up; the blood wasn't satisfying him like it usually did. He needed to up his game. Maybe he'd look into torture devices, see how far he could push the human body before it snapped. That could be amusing.

He rolled to a stop outside Lincoln Hospital and spotted the dark-haired beauty he'd been following for a few days. She was magnificent. Black hair and pure white skin. He longed to touch her, to bring her skin to life with a few crimson drops of blood. He felt himself grow hard in his jeans and shifted to accommodate the bulge. He didn't just want that woman, he *wanted* her. Maybe that's the piece that was missing for him, completely claiming his victims as his. Noting the deserted parking lot, he decided it was as good a time as any to make his move. Marcus could kiss his ass. There was no way he was stopping now when he was so close to discovering a new way to satisfy his urges.

He pulled his ski mask onto his head and left it rolled up, ready to pull down when he got close enough to her. He approached from the left side, careful to stay a few steps back until he was ready to make his move. She seemed to be pacing, no doubt waiting for someone to join her and if that was the case, he had to act fast. He pulled the mask down and grabbed her from behind. His strong arm went around her throat, cutting off her air; his other hand clamping down over her mouth, effectively cutting off any attempts she might make to scream.

"Hello, darling. I'd like you to come with me, please." he spoke into her ear as he dragged her to his car and opening the back door, shoved her in. It was an old-style cop car that only opened from the outside so all of her banging and crashing did her no good; she'd only tire herself out.

Just as he was about to climb into the driver's side, a second brunette woman emerged from the hospital, looking around. She must have caught movement out of the corner of her eye as she looked over and saw his captive trapped in the backseat, banging on the windows like they were drums.

"Hey!" she yelled and raced towards them. He planted his feet and let her come, not worried in the slightest. The second she got within arm's length of him, his fist shot out and he clocked her in the eye, watching as she hit the ground like a ton of bricks, knocked out cold. With a sigh, he picked her up and deposited her in the car as well.

"Looks like I got a two for one deal. Not bad."

Athena's head was pounding when she opened her eyes and she had a brief moment to think that she'd need to take some aspirin before heading into work. Something felt off and when she raised her head and looked around, she realized she wasn't home in her bed at all. She was in some sort of a basement. And she wasn't alone. At least a half dozen girls were down there with her, all restrained and some looked quite injured, blood seeping out from several wounds.

A moan off to her left had her turning her head and her eyes widened when she saw Sabine laying on the concrete floor, feet chained to a rail.

"Sab? Sabine, can you hear me?" she called out frantically. Fuck, where the hell were they? She vaguely remembered making plans to take a walk around the hospital gardens with Sabine on their break to choose a spot to plant a memorial tree for Sebastian. When she'd stepped outside, Sabine was nowhere to be found. Something had caught the corner of her eye and she saw her being transported away in a car by some guy in a mask. Not thinking, she'd raced over to try and stop him instead of going for help. That's the last thing she remembered. It seemed all she'd done was get them both landed in hot water.

"Thene? Where the hell are we?" Sabine demanded as she sat up. Her eyes took in the scene in the basement in horror and Athena knew what she must have looked like when she first saw the girls all chained up. They both yanked on their restraints, Athena's hands were chained together and to the same pipe that Sabine's feet were chained to. No amount of tugging was going to get them to break; they'd have to think of something else.

Athena studied the girls a little more closely. Their clothes were ragged and torn, their hair limp and greasy. Some of them, their ribs were poking out. These girls had been trapped for quite some time and obviously had not been cared for in any way. The cuts and gashes were in serious jeopardy of getting infected if they didn't get medical attention soon.

"I have no idea. But we need to get the fuck out of here, we all do." One of the girls off to the right let out a humorless laugh.

"Good luck with that. There's two of them you know. One just doesn't give a shit about us and the other one is far too fucking interested in us. They're insane, both of them. Crazy fucking fuckheads."

"Well I'd prefer the term, slightly unhinged, but to each their own I suppose." A man's voice answered as two feet came into view on the stairway directly in front of Sabine and Athena. Once he got to the bottom, she saw that he was tall, well built and wearing jeans and a black t-shirt. His facial features were a mystery due to the ski mask pulled over his face. He stopped a few feet away from them and crouched down so that they were eye level. His were a light brown from what she could see but that was the only identifying feature she could make out due to the mask. The fact that he seemed so at ease with what they were doing in this basement of horrors sent real terror through Athena's bones. There didn't seem to be a lick of remorse or regret in him.

"Why are we here?" Sabine asked, always the one to jump straight to the point.

"Why? That's an interesting question and not one anyone has asked before. Usually it's been, when can I go home or why won't you let me go. So you've intrigued me with your inquisition there, gorgeous. I think I'll show you though, instead of tell you." He rose to his feet once more and from the back of his jeans withdrew a large, menacing looking knife. Athena sucked in her breath, and kept her eyes glued to the blade, fear sliding through her over the thought of just what he planned on doing to show them why they were there.

Instead of slicing into them like she'd been afraid he was going to do, he walked over to the girl that had spoken to her and called them insane.

"You know, I don't think I liked your tone earlier, sugar. You had some not so nice things to say about me and my partner to our two lovely new guests. That was rather rude, don't you think?"

"I'm sorry. I'm s—s—sorry. It won't happen again. Please, just please don't cut me again. It hurts so bad," she begged, shrinking away as far she could by her restrained hands.

"Oh, now don't you fret. I'm not going to cause you any pain at all," he reassured her. Athena could hear her sigh of relief from across the room but it was quickly cut off by echoing screams as the man raised the knife and slashed her throat open, splaying blood everywhere. The girl slumped forward into the man and he coated his hands with the crimson liquid.

"See, bet you didn't even feel a thing."

chapter twenty

CIAN HADN'T SEEN Athena all day since she'd ran into him in the OR and seen more than she should have. Since then, she seemed to have fallen off the face of the earth and taken Sabine with her. It was a mystery and he was starting to get concerned as it wasn't like her to disappear in the middle of a shift. His girl was responsible and level-headed and cared too much about her patients to do something like that. *His girl?* Since when had he started referring to her as his girl?

He headed to the interns' locker room to once again see if they were there, disappointed when all he found was the other three. Fuckface whatever his name was, Clarence and Oscar were standing around chatting, getting ready to call it a day.

"Have you guys seen Athena and Sabine lately?" he asked, hating that he needed to, but not having any other choice.

"You know, I haven't seen either of them since this morning, now that you mention it," Clarence replied, scratching his head. Oscar also said no and Fuckface just shrugged.

"That's not an answer," Cian told him, stepping farther into the locker room.

"Look, I don't stick my nose in other people's business okay? If those two girls want to go riding off with some creepy looking dude, that's their deal and I want no part of it. I'm here to do my job and that's it," Dick told him, starting to walk around him to head for the door.

Cian's arm shot out and grabbing him by the throat, slammed him against the wall. "What the fuck are you talking about? Riding off with who? What creepy guy?" he demanded. He applied more pressure when Dick refused to answer. His face turned red and his eyes started to bug out before he nodded, indicating that he would talk. Cian loosened his grip but still held him firmly in place.

"Spill it," he ordered him.

"I happened to be walking by the front entrance when I saw Sabine in the back of some dude's car and Athena draped all over the same guy climbing in the front. The guy was wearing some kind of a hat; I couldn't really see his face from how far away I was but I thought it was odd. It looked like a winter hat and we sure as hell don't need to be wearing those in this heat. Anyways, he helped her in and then they sped off and I went on with my business."

"He helped her in the car from the *driver's side?* And he was wearing some kind of a winter mask? What time was this at?"

"I don't know. I guess it was around noon."

"Noon?! That was six hours ago and you didn't tell anybody! The guy was wearing a fucking ski mask; you shit for brain idiot!" Disgusted he shoved Dick towards the door. "Go to the nurses' station and get them to call the police. Now. Tell them two women have been abducted from Lincoln Hospital and we suspect the serial killers are involved. Move it!" he yelled when Dick hesitated, glaring at him until he stumbled out the door. Cian's head swam with a thousand different scenarios as panic gripped him. Why the fuck hadn't he noticed she was missing sooner? Where the hell would that sick bastard have taken her? If anything happened and he lost her...his heart couldn't bear to think of what could happen to her. He was going to get her back. He had to.

"You." He pointed to Clarence. "I've heard things about you. That you're good with computers. Can you track Athena's phone?"

"Um...I can try. But only if she still has it on," Clarence clarified, not wanting to commit to something he might not be able to do.

"Good, let's go, we need to move fast. They've already had them for hours." He shuddered at the thought of what might have happened to Athena. If they'd harmed even one hair on her head...

"In here," he ushered both Clarence and Oscar into his office. Clarence immediately jumped on the computer and Cian rattled off the number of her cell phone. He stared at the screen expectantly, hoping something would magically pop up that would tell him her whereabouts.

"Her phone is off," Clarence told him, cowering in case he decided to take the news out on him. "But wait. I might be able to get a signal off her last known tower ping." His fingers flew over the keys as he tapped away. It all looked like gibberish to Cian but every now and then, he made a small grunt that sounded like it might be good news.

"Well?" he prodded, unable to take it anymore.

"Shhh, give me a minute," Clarence ordered and then froze. "Uh, sir. Give me a minute, sir. Please?"

"Yeah, yeah, just hurry the fuck up."

Ten minutes later, just as Cian was ready to strangle the fuck out of Clarence, he looked up with a grin.

"I got an address. I pinged the last closest location and from that I cross referenced who in the area rented properties recently and only came up with one hit. 421 53rd St. Rented to a Dr. Daniels three weeks ago. This has to be the place." Clarence announced triumphantly.

"Great. Call the cops and tell them," he said as he ran out the door. He was frantic to get to her, waiting for the police was not an option. There's no way they would go in there guns blazin', but he sure as fuck would. His only priority was Athena and getting her out safely, everyone else was the cops' responsibility.

Pulling up to the condo, he leaped from the car and went to sprint up the condo's front steps, only to collide with another man. Each stepped back and glared at the other.

"Who the fuck are you?" they asked each other at the same time and then frowned.

"I'm Gabe Thornton. I don't think you want to go in there. This house is not what you think."

"I'm Dr. Cian O'Reilly. And I sure as fuck am going in there. My woman is in there and I need to get her out and to safety." The two men regarded each other and deciding that each wasn't the bad guy, backed down a bit.

"I'm here for Marcus Drake," Gabe told him.

"I don't know who that is, I'm here for Athena and Sabine. They're being held in there."

Gabe nodded. "Probably by Marcus. Look, I'll have your back in there if you'll have mine, just don't get in my way when I kill that son-of-a-bitch."

"Agreed. Don't get in mine if I kill anyone that's laid a hand on my woman."

The two shook hands and approached the door together. "Cops will be here soon. Whatever we're gonna do, we have maybe ten minutes before they're all over this place," Cian told him.

"Got it. Let's do this."

Cian kicked in the door and the two separated, each searching rooms on either side of the front entrance. When they came up empty, the reunited in the hallway and Gabe signaled that he was going upstairs while Cian took the kitchen and other lower rooms. When they still came up empty-handed several minutes later, he began to panic thinking that Clarence had been all wrong about the address.

Gabe waved him over and pointed and that's when he spotted the door to the basement. It was reinforced with several locks on the outside which was a dead giveaway that something was down there the occupants of the house didn't want getting free.

They had a silent argument of who was going first, eventually have to resort to Rock, Paper, Scissors. Gabe won, much to Cian's dismay and he descended the stairs first, with Cian taking up the rear.

Halfway down the stairs, they heard the screams and cries. Nothing could have prepared them for the scene before their eyes.

A half dozen women were being held captive; some suspended from the ceiling by chains, others on the floor with longer chains attached to their hands or feet. All were covered in multiple cuts and gashes and looked like they hadn't been fed in weeks. There was a commotion over in the left corner and glancing over, Cian spotted a man towering over Athena and Sabine, attempting to drag an unconscious Sabine away while Athena tried to fight him off.

"Jesus, fuck. It's Dr. Daniels," Gabe muttered. Cian had no idea who Dr. Daniels was, but Gabe was obviously not a fan as he charged at him and tackled him to the ground, feeding him punch after punch.

Cian rushed over and snatched Athena into his arms. "Are you okay? Are you hurt? Did he cut you?" He looked her over from head to toe, trying to find injuries.

"I'm okay, I'm okay, but Cian, please. Get us out of here before he comes back. He cut Sabine bad on her arm and she passed out. And h—h—he killed one of the other girls just for talking to us. Please get us out of here."

"I will, baby. Just try to stay calm. He had no keys for the cuffs she was wearing and that fucking pissed him off. He spotted a saw over in the corner and grabbed it, intent on cutting through the chains. Gabe had finally stopped whaling on Dr. Daniels and from the state of his bashed in face; he was dead.

He walked over and took the saw from Cian. "Here, man, I'll get that."

"Athena, where are the men that brought you here?" She shook her head, still in shock over what they'd been through.

"There was only one man. He killed that girl and then he cut Sabine when she smart-mouthed him. I thought he was going to kill us too. He escaped—" she pointed to a small cellar door in the corner. "—out that door when he heard you guys upstairs. He was furious...so much rage." Her whole body started to quake and Cian pulled her into his arms again. The sirens wailed in the distance just as Gabe got finished cutting through Athena's chains. The other women in the room started crying tears of relief that they'd been found and it was all too much. The despair and torture in that basement was sickening. She was so lucky that Cian found her before she was subjected to anything like they'd endured.

"Take us home, Cian. Please just take us home."

chapter twenty-one

ATHENA SPENT THE three days after her rescue tucked into bed at Cian's apartment. He'd insisted she stay with him after everything that had happened and too exhausted to think, she hadn't argued with him. He'd been patient and kind with her the entire time, making sure she had everything she needed at all times. If she hadn't already fallen for him, she would have during those few days. The man that they had met, Gabe, had disappeared almost immediately after all the girls had been freed, not wanting to be involved with the police. Apparently his hunt for this Marcus person was his own personal vendetta and not one sanctioned by the authorities. Cian seemed to really understand his reasoning, which confused her but she let it go.

He was distant with her but attentive at the same time and it was driving her mental. She could tell there was something on his mind, something that was eating at him and had him pacing the apartment like a caged cat.

"Cian," she called out to him one evening after watching him circle past the bedroom door for the fifth time. "Please come in and tell me what's bothering you. You're driving me mad."

He sighed and crossed the room to sit beside her. She moved back until she was in his arms and could lay her head on his chest. She felt safe and protected; exactly what she needed.

"I've been going over this for a few weeks now. It's finally time I share my past with you and open up about who I am, Athena. If we're going to do this for real, you deserve to know the truth about everything." Her olive eyes were trained on him, so expressive and full of love and trust. If he hadn't already fallen for her then he would have in the next moment when she laid her hand over his heart and spoke softly to him.

"I already know everything I need to know about you, Cian. You're a good, kind man. You're the man I love."

He pressed his lips to hers in a hard kiss, feeling more alive in that moment than he had in years. "I love you too, Athena. Please remember that." She nodded and slipped her hand in his, encouraging him to tell her whatever was on his mind.

"I was married once...her name was Hannah and she was the joy of my life." He walked her through their life together and what happened on that fateful day when she was stolen from him. His heart filled with more love for her when her eyes filled with tears that spilled down her cheeks when he laid out in detail how she was stolen from him.

"Cian. I'm so, so sorry. I can't even imagine the pain you must have felt losing her."

"I didn't lose her. She was stolen from me, and that's a wrong I plan to make right one day." He saw her puzzled expression and took a deep breath before continuing.

"There's something else I need to tell you. Something that I do, that I'm a part of. Athena, I hunt criminals. Criminals that have somehow escaped the justice system and ended up back on the streets. Scum of the earth like the men who killed my wife. People that are in need of killing. I hunt them, I bring them to my OR and I dispose of them once and for all. I am their justice. Their executioner. I'm the monster they have nightmares about. Once they end up in my OR, their sins become mine to avenge. And I do avenge them, Athena, in brutal, terrible ways. I make them suffer just as they made their victims suffer. I'm their Hell on earth."

Athena was silent for a long while, processing what he'd told her. He kept quiet and let her think, but with each passing second he feared she was pulling away from him. When she finally looked up at him, he saw the change in her eyes.

"I want to be a part of your team. Teach me, Cian. Teach me how it is to serve justice to those that deserve it. I'm ready."

epilogue

DANE CLIMBED OUT of his car and walked along the dirt path to the deserted warehouse he was meeting his contact at. Since the disaster in New York, he and Marcus had decided that it was best they say their goodbyes and go their separate ways. Neither needed the other anymore and working together was causing more friction than it was worth.

Dane had his own plans and was anxious to see them come into play. Spotting the lone figure standing in the doorway to the warehouse, he made his way to the entrance and followed him inside. He looked around the building, nodding approvingly.

"This should do nicely. Good work."

Oscar Breyers turned to face him and flashed a cold smile. "Thanks, boss. I can't wait to get this place up and running. It's pretty amazing what an intern and a cop can do once they put their heads together, isn't that right, Detective Seth Holloway?"

Dane let out a laugh and held up his hands. "Hey, that cover was working just fine until recently. Got my head messed up over a damn female, but I'm straightened out now. And I'm more than ready for my revenge. I want you to keep up spying and leaking information on O'Reilly. When the time is right, we'll make them all suffer."

THE END

acknowledgements

Jerzie, Charlee, Jessica – This book meant so much to me to write and I couldn't have done it without the three of you. Thank you for being there for me through all of my up's and down's...I truly love you guys so much.

Toni Thompson – I couldn't ask for a better PA and friend. You're always supporting me and making me laugh when I need it the most. You're truly amazing and I can't wait to see what awesome things happen for you this year. THANK YOU! xoxo

River Savage, Gilly Jones, Alissa Evanson Smith – There isn't even words to say how much I love you three. Our daily chats are what I look forward to the most and I love how we have each other's backs no matter what. Bring on Cleveland! Can't wait to get our tattoos xoxo

Lance Jones – You've become one of my bestest friends! I'm so lucky to be partners with you and can't wait for all the exciting things we have planned for our businesses this year. Thank you for everything and all the support xoxo

Brendan James – You rocked this cover for me! I love it so much and I'm so grateful that we met in New York and it worked out for us to work together. You're pretty awesome and a great friend, looking forward to more to come in the future!

Judi Perkins – You are amazing, lady. Thank you for putting up with my endless changes to LH's cover and making it

what I envisioned. I'm so lucky to call you one of my best friends –
thank you for being you! xoxo

   To My Betas – You ladies rock my world and I'm so
grateful to have you! Thank you for working with me and helping
me bring my writing up to the level I want it to be on. You're
amazing, all of you.

   Sirens – This is my favorite place in the world. My safe
place, my comfort zone. I love how each of us supports each other
and that we have a place to escape and be ourselves and share our
love of books. You're my biggest cheerleaders and I couldn't be
more grateful for each and every one of you.

   To My Family – I'm a lucky girl to have such an amazing
family. You support me through all of this, through my goals and
ambitions and offer me guidance when I need it to see the end
result come to light. Thank you for all the love and encouragement
through one of our toughest years. I love you all so much.

   To The Book Community – Being an indie author isn't an
easy thing. It takes true hard work and dedication. The friends
that I've made, the readers and fellow authors that I've met on this
journey—I cherish you all and I'm so grateful for the support I've
received. Just one PM message can make someone's day and every
one that I receive warms my heart more than you know. Thank
you for taking a chance on my work even when it's more twisted
than expected lol ;)

about the author

Cassia Brightmore is a dark romance author. She loves writing dark stories with twisted characters that she hopes will thrill the reader as well as make them fall in love.

She loves hockey, video games and online shopping. If she's not writing or editing, you can usually find her doing one of these things. Writing is her passion and publishing her first book as an indie author is truly a dream come true.

Cassia lives in Ontario, Canada with her two furbabies; Molly and Harley.

Her titles include:

The Darkness Series
Book One: Malevolent
Book Two: Evanesce
Book Three: Denouement
Book Four: Repentance

To look for in 2016:

New Dark Romance Standalone: Unworthy, expected release: June, 2016
New Dark Romance Standalone: Mercenary, expected release: September, 2016

CONNECT WITH CASSIA

LINCOLN HOSPITAL

TWITTER - INSTAGRAM - PINTEREST - FACEBOOK - WEBSITE
cassiabrightmore@gmail.com

JOIN CASSIA'S FAN GROUP:
https://www.facebook.com/groups/CassiasSassySirens/

32803493R00114

Made in the USA
Middletown, DE
19 June 2016